Nocturne Chocolate

by

Duncan Eastman

+

Rachel Frichette

Part 1:
Fanfare

Rhapsody

There are very few sensations one experiences in her life that can even attempt to compare with my current flood of emotions. After many a wretched day spent in this foreboding hellhole, fighting for my life day after day, and never knowing quite when the next strike below the belt might rear its treacherous head, I am free. The feeling, just so the regular folk of the world can begin to understand my relief, is that of walking tediously through a desert for days on end, with the hope of food or water all but banished from your feeble imagination, the sun baking your skin to resemble crisp bacon that one's mother might make on a holiday morning, and your legs the consistency of said fried swine before said frying has commenced. After this exhausting and painful journey, when there's seemingly no end in sight, out of the surrounding ocean of sand, in a whirlpool of "Hallelujah" and "Praise Jesus" rises a building holier and more hospitable than them all. A Costco. In this Costco, which is, of course, air conditioned to a perfectly brisk 69 degrees (And no, not Celsius, my Canadian acquaintances), you find endless samples to snack on to your heart's content, and a line of thirty water fountains, waiting to be guzzled at. Thus was my relief as I woke this particular morning to the smell of, yes indeed, the aforementioned "mother's fried swine".

Such fried swine only presented itself on special occasions, and as I would remember momentarily, after the mouthwatering aroma cleared the muddle headedness gathered from a solid ten hours of sleep, this morning was no exception. For this, my dear friends, was the day of my high school graduation, and time to start living.

Today, a Thursday, mediocre, I'm sure, for

everyone past the age of eighteen, warranted a showtune. Despite the overcast sky (In June. Honestly, Portland? Can't bother to overcome the clouds for my ONE special day?), the strain of flu laying siege to my family of five (Yep, two younger brothers. Go ahead and feel sorry for me. I certainly take the time to on a regular basis.), and the complete lack, as I would soon discover, of control over the television (Damned 12 year old boys have an uncanny ability to always, without fail, get up before their sister and, thus, claim the TV remote), this was going to prove to be one of the single best days of my entire life. I could feel it. "Oh, What A Beautiful Mornin'" indeed.

After sufficient singing in the shower, the bathroom acoustics making me sound like the Idina Menzel that I am, and a hurried dressing ritual I'd perfected with years of practice (due to my lack of knowledge in the category of style, or care of it, for that matter, I can pick out an entire outfit in under fifteen rushed seconds with my eyes closed.), I emerge into the already alive living room, mismatched from head to toe, just as it should be.

The scene I am presented with is one of American cliche, to say the least. My mother, the beautiful, albeit heavy set, Dinah Buchanan (Yep, named after Dinah Washington), stands in the kitchen, complete with red apron, sweating over the stove as the second batch of bacon (If there is a God, that bastard presents himself to the general public in the form of my mom's bacon) is being divided equally among four plates, which becomes five quickly when my mom catches sight of me in the corner of her eye "Morning, Ella!" she shouts without looking up from her work.

The couch in front of the TV, just like the TV itself, has been completely taken over by my two younger brothers, Louis and Duke. Even on my SPECIAL DAY, I'm going to be forced to sit through reruns of Star Trek. And not even the new ones. The damned original one. Or as Trekkies, such as my father and brothers, call it, "Star Trek TOS". As if the acronym makes it less nerdy.

Now would probably be a good time to explain that the Buchanan family is by no means religious. However, this fact does not mean we do not have religions. In this household, the religions are as follows, in ascending order of importance.

1). Food. The first thing people notice about us on a snap judgment is that we're not thin. We're not technically overweight, due to the quality of the foods involved in our mass consumption, but we're definitely not skinny. We're somewhat infamous for planning interactions with those outside the family around the schedules of our favorite restaurants. "Hey Ella, want to go to a movie this weekend? Maybe Saturday at seven or eight?" a friend might ask. At this point in the conversation, I am forced to shoot such a friend down because "Sorry, but that conflicts with the Peak of Performance at Andina".
The Peak of Performance, or POP, is something my family uses to keep track of when to eat at a particular food spot. Andina, a candlelit Peruvian tapas bar, starts dinner at 4, and closes at 11. Can't go too early, or else you get the uptight hipster families (of which there are many in Portland) laughing too noisily about jokes that they wrote while backpacking in Europe or something. Best to stay away from them. Go too late, however, and you get drunks, laughing much too noisily at, well, everything. However, you want to be as late as possible in the evening, so the cooks have established a groove, but are not yet exhausted from a long shift. Thus, a reasonable POP for Andina is a soft 8 o'clock. See what I mean? The Buchanans take matters such as these very seriously, so it's no fault of ours that the bathroom scale is not what you'd call flattering.

2). Star Trek. Now, as I've pointed out, I'm not quite as hot on this topic as my darling (NERDY) brothers and father. I appreciate it enough to laugh at Captain Kirk's witty humor and melodramatic acting, but I draw the line at the annual invitation I get from them to drive down to

Comic-con, dressed as the crew of the Enterprise. I also exclude myself from the annual argument of who gets to be Spock, which Duke has won the last two years, by threatening not to go if he has to be Scotty. Louis always concedes to this because going with only a Spock and Kirk "would make us look lame". Sure, that would make it lame.

Over the past couple years, it's become commonplace to communicate, especially at the dinner table (where it is least difficult to annoy their older sister) in geek speak. Those boys are both getting B minuses in English, yet they're fluent in Klingon. What does that tell you about our society?

3). Jazz. Now this one is one we all worship. If you hadn't guessed from our names, our parents are what you might call enthusiasts of jazz. Dinah (Again, named after Dinah Washington) got this obsession from her parents, met my dad, Cab (Named for Cab Calloway), who got the obsession from his parents. Of course, this mutual obsession made them fall madly in love and have 20 pounds of babies, who they, in turn, spread their obsession to. I, of course, am named after dearest Ella Fitzgerald, while the brothers are named after Louis Armstrong and Duke Ellington. Just as it's no secret that my family has a bit too much of the roundness about the middle, it's even less of a secret that our appearances do not fit our names. Ella, Duke, Louis, Cab, and Dinah? Seem to be rather black names, don't they? Well, the Buchanans couldn't be whiter. Nevertheless, jazz is our favorite thing on the planet, and it shows.

Each of us, per our parents' wishes, is 110% musical. All of us sing, all of us play the piano, and all of us got to pick a wind instrument to learn. The flute and alto sax slots were already filled by father and mother, respectively, so when the question was popped on my ninth birthday, I set my sights on a clarinet, while my brothers, 5 years later, settled on their instruments, Duke on trombone/trumpet and Louis on tenor sax.. We're basically the swing version of the Von Trapp family. Minus the Nazis, of course.

Today, being the final day of school, ends my dreadful four years of high school and, of course, warranted celebration of the highest proportion, indulging as many of our religions as is humanly possible. Giving a day concert for the high school graduation with the rest of the Buchanan Family Band by the day, a wonderful (albeit costly) dinner at my favorite restaurant at its peak of performance, and between the two, the boys of the family will be gone, at a showing of the new Star Trek movie. This day...will...be...awesome...

Bourbon Street

<u>Journal Entry 1</u>
October 14th, 2012

I never thought I would actually find myself writing in a journal, but after this month I needed to write out what exactly is going on in my aching head so I can begin to decipher this recently developed feeling. This is something I have not experienced and I'm not so sure what it is precisely. Jotting these thoughts down may just help me alleviate and figure myself out and all the incertitude that takes place in my intellect especially with such desolation I had felt after this month. September 12th, 2012 is where this had begun and I'm not quite sure if there will ever be an end, but who knows? Maybe this is just my mind playing an evil trick on me.

I cannot quite grasp on to why I won't talk to Jimmy about this. Nothing about him seems right lately and my anger towards him continues to build faintly stronger and stronger. He's honestly a pretty average man so it wouldn't make any sense why I have these concerns about him. He's a director in his mid-30's, 34 or 35 maybe, but I don't quite know because I honestly couldn't care less. He tends to be overly proud about everything he does, but I always appreciated that about him. He has self confidence unlike many people and well, of course, myself. We met 5 or so years ago as I was playing my sax, "Red" (yes, I name my instruments, but we'll get to that later.) on the crowded streets of Seattle. He walked up to me and said something along the lines of "Hi, I'm Jimmy Atwell, a director in the Seattle area. You play beautifully and if you are interested I may have a way of getting you to play for one of my shows". The rest is kind of a blur. Here's the thing, I don't play for money. I play to give people different perspectives on such an art. I rejected his offer and he kept trying. Eventually we ended up agreeing on playing together for some odd reason. I'm not really sure how it ended up at that, but it did. We now play in my favorite coffee shop, Ground Zero (get it?), just about every Sunday. While I jam on piano or sax, he plays trombone. Occasionally we plan something and practice a bit, but most of the time we tend to just go with the flow. We never really decided on a name for our duo, so we just go by Quentin Harris and Jimmy Atwell. We have always had so much fun working together up until about a month ago.

Last month I started experiencing odd nightmares about hurting Jimmy, no one else except him. It makes absolutely no sense. One day we're having a casual latte on the street corner of 6th avenue at Ground Zero and the next I can hardly stand seeing him. Did he say something? Did he do something wrong? There had to have been some sort of reasoning behind this. I will find out, I have to. Whatever this is, it's taking over me piece by piece and if I don't figure it out soon, I will no longer be Quentin George Harris. I will be pure evil. I will be something I never wanted to be. I must figure this out, sooner rather than later, but how will I? Honestly, the real question is, will I ever?

Rhapsody ii

"Ladies, gentlemen, and those who have yet to make up your minds", I laugh to myself as I address my graduating class.

"This has been, without a doubt in my mind, the best four years of my life (lie), and I don't think I would be able to even think such a statement if I had not had all of you by my side (lie again). Although we don't know what tomorrow will bring, or what we have encountered in our individual yesterdays, all of our futures, I know, will end in success (Wow, I lie a lot...). I know this hasn't been the best year for all of you, but I just want you to know how much you've accomplished. Graduating is not as easy as most people think. Your parents had it easier, and your younger siblings don't even know what's coming. Only you can understand how monumental of an achievement this really is. And you should all feel so proud to have overcome such a mountain. You should feel good. Really good." I tap my foot to indicate to my family, standing behind me, the tempo of the upcoming piece.

"I know I'm feeling good."

The sting of a high hat behind me, played by my mother, marks my time as I begin to sing a Capella.

"Birds flying high, you know I feel."

I see smiles exchanged around the audience as my voice echoes throughout the stadium and the recognition of this amazing song brings goosebumps to every graduating senior listening. "Sun in the sky, you know I feel. Br-e-e-ze..." I let the piercing note hang in the air for a full beat of rest before I continue.

"...drifting on by, you know how I feel. It's a new dawn, it's a new day, it's a new life...for me..." I nod at my father and brothers and they raise their instruments as I hit my last phrase before their entrance.

"...and I'm feeling good." As the boys blast on their brass, I step away from the microphone to give them their moment. As the instrumental section blazes up the ears of the audience, I take a second to scan the crowd, see if there's anyone I haven't seen before. I pride myself in my photographic memory, and I've probably laid eyes on almost everyone in Portland at some point, so an unfamiliar face is a somewhat rare occasion. The faces so far, halfway through my scan, are completely recognizable, until I lay eyes on a rather attractive man standing apart from the staff, but not sitting with the seniors.

Said man is too old to be a student here, even if he was held back three times. However, he doesn't look so old that I'd be inclined to identify him as a parent. The suit also sets him apart. He looks like a business owner or something, complete with a bluetooth earpiece. Not focusing on his stuck-up appearance, I might even call him attractive, which is a high honor from Ella Buchanan.

I'm so focused on the man, I almost miss my next entrance. As I belt the easy notes, I can't take my eyes off of him.

"Fish in the sea..."

He's started staring at me. Shit.

"...you know how I feel."

Okay, now he's smiling, still staring. Ugh.

"River running free..."

Wow, he's attractive...

"...you know how I feel"

Can he stop staring at me? Jesus...

"Blossom on the tree..."

This continues for the rest of the song. The two of us, locked in eye contact, unwavering from our focus. As the song comes to a dramatic close, and the boys chop out on high notes to strike a screeching final chord, the crowd of seniors erupts in applause and I bow, acknowledging my family with a wave of my arm. Still, the man can't stop looking at me. I mean, I am gorgeously wonderful and whatnot, but still.

***

"So, you're Ella Buchanan?" I nod to the man as I shake his outstretched hand.

After finishing Feelin' Good, he had intercepted me on my way to the ladies' room, and had not yet introduced himself. "Yes, indeed. And you are?"
A slight wince flashes across his face as my handshake briefly crushes his hand (I always attempt to be firm.).

"Atwell. James Atwell." He says with a smirk. What a flirt, Jesus.

"But call me Jimmy". Another smirk.

I raise one eyebrow as I inquire about him. "Well, Jimmy. You're at a high school graduation, making eyes at an 18 year old, an age which you are clearly not, and I want an explanation."

"I'm not making eyes at you, don't worry. I'm purely interested in that voice of yours. Goddamn, you've got great vibrato control for someone your age and your low register is just...wow..."

Nothing I haven't heard before. I know I'm good. I wouldn't sing in front of my entire class if I didn't know it.

"Anyway, I'm a director."

Now he's got my attention.

"Should've started with that line, big boy." I return his toothy smirk.

He chuckles, removing the earpiece and pocketing it. "I'm doing a production of Rent up in the Seattle area. I've had an easy time finding every part, except for Maureen. I've held three auditions and I'm just not satisfied with what I see, so I decided to start scouting. I know the role is a little old for you,"

As if that would stop me.
"but from what I just heard, you could definitely take it on. We're opening for a month at the 5th Avenue theatre, and if it's successful, we'll start touring around the west coast. As far as I'm concerned, that song you just sang was your audition and, sweetheart, you blew

me away. I want you to be my Maureen. You in?"
Holy shit. My mind is exploding. Yes, yes, yes!!! A MILLION TIMES YES!!! BROADWAY MUSICALS??? HELL YES!!!

"Um...sure!" I'm smooth, I know.

"That's wonderful, Ella!" He hugs me. I hate hugs. My stiff body makes the hug so uncomfortable, he pulls away after about a second.

"How long will it take you to pack? I can set you up in an apartment in Seattle until you can support yourself, so all you need is clothes."

"Give me half an hour to pack, and then I'll talk to my family about it and say my temporary goodbyes and all that."

I check my phone. 2:34. "I'll be ready by six."

***

Obviously the news came as a shock to my family. I hadn't committed to any colleges yet, because I planned to stick with my family and play with them until the boys got into high school in a year, so they weren't prepared to say goodbye yet. Even my little brothers were sad to say farewell to their big sister which makes me pretty damn grateful. Most little brothers would be the first to say "don't let the door hit you on the way out" to their big sister, but not Louis and Duke. You develop a certain connection when you play music together.

Contrary to the time I had planned out, it only takes me 22 minutes to pack all the clothes I will need, due to my expert packing skills. Given, most of the clothes are jeans and t-shirts, neatly wrinkled together in a duffel bag. But still, that must be a record or something.

I keep hearing Jimmy's (that name makes him sound like such a tool, my god) voice over and over in my head. I want you to be my Maureen. You in? I always expected to have a jazz career, but Broadway musicals is

completely unprecedented. But now that I am actually on my way, I start to understand that this has my name written all over it. And Rent, even! That show seems to be written for me. Take Me Or Leave Me has been covered by my mother and I so many times that I could probably sing it deaf and still be pitch perfect.
The final goodbyes are teary, of course. I even cry. However, I can't be too sad. I'm gonna be Maureen!

As I get in the car to leave for Seattle, to the address of Jimmy's apartment (he's letting me stay at his place until he can secure an apartment for me), a huge smile breaks through the wall of tears rushing down my face. I am actually doing this. I'm making it big, in a big show, in a big city, with a big apartment, and a big ego I think to myself.

I take it as a sign of success when I turn on my car's stereo and my favorite song is the first sound to blast my ears.

"...and I'm feelin'..."

Ladies and gentlemen, give it up for...Ella Buchanan!
"..good."

My Old Heart

Journal Entry 2

October 29th, 2012

It felt like everything was slowly fading into a black hole. Like my thoughts and feelings were beginning to fall endlessly down a pit to nowhere, but something changed that. I met a girl. Well, I technically haven't met her, but she's more perfect than anything perfect can be. I don't know her name, her age, her favorite book, her favorite movie. I didn't need to know right now. She was the most beautiful thing I have ever seen and one day, I hope to bump into her again. I will find out her name, I promise.

I was playing outside the 5th Avenue on my sax, "Red", and heard a yelling coming from the inside as she was walking out. I looked to my left and there she was, tears in her eyes as if she had been hurt so badly she could barely breathe. I stopped playing and was mesmerized by her. I wanted to go up to her, comfort her, but the minute I put my eyes on her, the world stopped. Her skin pale as snow, her hair as brown as the trunks of the evergreen trees, cheeks mildly red from all the tears flowing from her sparkling brown eyes. Not a single trace of makeup lay upon her face. Everything I saw was pure beauty and I was absolutely amazed by it.

I wanted to know what was wrong, if I could help in any way possible. I wanted to know what man hurt her because hearing the yelling I could tell that it was a man's voice. Well, it could have been a very manly woman because you never know, but I'm 90% sure it was a man. Whoever made her cry that hard deserves punishment. They need to pay for hurting her.

Why do I have strong feelings for her when I don't even know the slightest thing about her? I want to know. I can't get her face out of my head. Every time I close my eyes, I see her, standing out in the cold, shivering, sobbing, while I stand a distance away watching and not doing a single thing to help. I was too scared. I was scared to approach her the wrong way, to ruin anything that can happen between us. It's like I actually knew her. The minute I saw her, it felt like I had known her for several years, as if she was a part of my life. I have never seen this girl before and I hope that one day I will see her again. Please.

Polonaise

I love curtain calls. Oh my sweet baby Jesus. There is nothing, absolutely nothing I have experienced in my life that gives me the same thrill and satisfaction. Better than bacon, better than Costco, and god knows it's better than sex. On the final curtain call of Rent six years ago, I even cried. Crazy right? I hadn't cried since I left home, so it was extremely shocking to me, as well as the members of the cast.

Rent was such a success across the west coast that, when Jimmy told me he was working on a new project, I just had to be involved. Turned out he was actually writing his own play, a murder mystery based on the assassination of Martin Luther King Jr., with a turn on the actual history of the event. This ran for a short 6 weeks before going completely bankrupt when it hit Portland. The exact opposite from the sweeping victory of Rent, the murder mystery, deemed King by Jimmy, was over before it began. This show was what would produce the worst reviews of my entire career, and cause Jimmy Atwell, loved by audiences across Washington, Oregon, and California, to fall into a two year long slump of being broke, drinking, a brief brush with drugs, not writing any more shows (thank god, it's obviously not his strong suit), and, most importantly, not directing.

Out of work, and out of the economical safety Jimmy had promised but I had not needed in years, I had to find something with which to pay the bills. Now, keep in mind that I had actually only been to one official audition, which was for a play, not a musical. Thus, the thought of actually auditioning for a full-on show was pretty nerve wracking.

Using Feelin' Good as my audition song (don't mess with success, right?), I auditioned for small shows all over the Seattle area for several months on end.

According to condescendingly insulting remarks from various directors, I have "too much of an aggressive personality for The Last 5 Years" (meaning I'm a diva), I "don't possess the right body figure for Les Miserables" (meaning I'm fat), and I "just don't have the right voice for Oklahoma!" (I'm trained in jazz, what do you expect?).

These months were the rock bottom of Ella Buchanan's life. I didn't have a job, I was pinching pennies, and, for the first time in my life, I was scared of what was to come. I was created and sculpted with a very specific skill set, and most directors, excluding the once great James Atwell, seemed to not take kindly to it. In the end, I settled to working at a coffee house until something better came along. The place was called Ground Zero (I really do hate puns). The coffee was decent, it payed a little above the minimum wage, and there was live music from time to time, so I decided it was better than the alternatives, the alternatives being stripping and selling drugs. This would be where I stayed for two years of my life. Cue the sympathy.

***

Given the circumstances, you'd probably guess when Jimmy came to me, after what seemed like an eternity of inactivity, with a new project, I would be somewhat skeptical. Well, you'd be wrong. Understanding that he obviously wasn't Shakespeare, he had decided to turn to a guaranteed hit for the critics. It's not a musical, a comedy, or in any means like anything I'd ever worked on before, but I'd been in this business at least long enough to know that Tennessee Williams' A Streetcar Named Desire was something I definitely, without a doubt, wanted to be involved in.
"I know I've asked you this before," he says after placing a very generous tip in my tip jar after taking a sip of a kickass macchiato, "but would you be interested in working with me again? I can help you pick out a

monologue if ya like, to help you get back in the game." I find it a bit unsettling that he knows I haven't performed since last time we worked together, but that's beside the point. I hadn't been on a stage in 800 days and that fact was getting a little taxing on my massive ego, slowly decreasing in size. I hadn't actually sung in so long, I was forgetting words to Feelin' Good. What the actual hell.

"Absolutely. As long as you're just directing." Believe me, after that steaming turd of a play, King, Jimmy would never live down the "you suck at writing" jokes, jabs, and insults.

"If I'm auditioning, what role am I auditioning for? Just so I can research how she's played and whatnot." Even though I knew the play was supposed to be amazing, I didn't know a damn thing about it.

"I'll tell you when you audition. I want you to just do your thing, coloring within the lines, of course, being that's it's set in the forties. Don't watch the movie, don't read what it's about, just go for it. You'll probably end up being the only actress there with a fresh perspective, which means you'll stand out. So I can easily have a reason to put you in."

"Fair enough." It felt a bit like a slap in the face that I had to have an agreement with the director to get into the show, but at this point, I didn't really care. "Give me a time and place, and I'll be there".

"5 PM at the 5th Ave."

"See you there."

***

Jimmy was right. The other women showing up to the auditions had resumes a half mile long, so when I showed up with two shows on the back of my head shot and no college experience, I stuck out like a sore thumb. My competition looked almost famous. Not that I recognized them or anything, but they just looked famous. Tall, thin, blonde, blue eyed, lipsticked, eyelinered, looking ready to conquer the world. Then there was me. Not tall, nor thin, brunette, brown eyed, with little to no makeup (once you have someone do your makeup for you every damn day for a couple years and you look like a freaking movie star, it's kinda hard to replicate results yourself. Thus, you sorta lose interest.), and not ready to conquer the bathroom, let alone the world.

As per Mr. Atwell's advice, I hadn't read through any synopses, nor watched any clips of the show. I was the only one here, at least I suspected, with no clue what she was doing. This should be interesting.

The first part of the audition was a session of cold reads (for those of you who don't know, that's when you get part of the script and have to read in character with other people, sort of improvising the blocking as you go. I absolutely hated it.) At least ten girls went before me (Yes. Girls. Not women. They all looked 23, and not a damn day older.), and all, as Jimmy had predicted, read the roles almost exactly the same. The first scene being used was a dialogue between a married couple in an abusive relationship, Stella and Stanley. Stella was always played with just a hint of stupidity, with a strong New Orleans accent, and she always tried to be able to smile at everything. Stanley was always played as a man that would drive around in a pickup truck with a confederate flag waving from the tailgate just to come home and beat his wife. As Jimmy saw this, his disappointment was clear. This is what he had known would happen with such a well known show. No new looks on the characters. Well, that was about to change.

"Ella Buchanan, read for Stella, and Danny Harris, read for Stanley." I grabbed a section of script from a stage manager as I bounced up onstage, in the way that I always do. Danny Harris was, to say the least, huge. Not fat, but not especially muscular, just enormous. At least seven inches taller than me, and probably weighed fifty percent more. Going into this, I knew I couldn't do a New Orleans accent, so I just did my natural Oregonian accent, and, by coincidence, Danny stuck to his roots as well. Throwing at least the characters' accent out the window, we went on to deliver the most original performance anyone had seen that day. I was not a dumb blonde. I reacted how I would react, and it felt wonderful. The words just flowed from my mouth as the two of us argued back and forth, a tenacity tango. When his voice would drop, mine would drop, when I shouted, he shouted louder. God, I love teamwork.

I can see why Jimmy wanted something fresh. If people were used to the Stella the girls had played, they were gonna be blown away by me. I was small, mighty, and ready to run. As we finished the scene, I shook Danny's hand before leaving the stage.

"Nice work, kind sir." I whispered.

"Thanks! Not too bad yourself, madam." He made me smile as he spoke.

Walking back to my seat, I got looks from the girls, that just screamed "Oh, it's that girl with no education" or "Wow, would it kill you to lose a few pounds, bitch?".

"When I get this damn part..." I think to myself, "Y'all can go fuck yourselves."

Turns out, I actually did get it. And so did Danny. Thus began the role that actually changed my life for the better, for the worse, and everything in between.

***

Two months into Streetcar Named Desire, after the second weekend of wonderful, perfect, performances had begun, I got a phone call. When I looked down to see my mom's name, I was immediately worried. My dad called me. My mom did not. Mom hates talking on the phone. We would Skype from time to time if she was in the mood, but the last time she called me was the day after I left for Seattle.

"Mom? Is everything okay?" I only hear sobbing.

Shit. Shit. Shit.

"MOM! What's wrong?!" More sobbing. My heart is

racing now, I break into a run trying to get off the street of 5th avenue and into the theatre, where I'll be able to hear every choked word. I've just set foot in the dark theatre when she utters her first words.

"Louis' dead." Whoa.

"You know he's been trying to pay his way through college...he...got in an accident at work..."

Oh my god. No no no no no no...

"...How?" I have to know.

"He was working in a mill. He," sob "never told us much about it because he didn't want us to worry..." Her words are speeding up and being crammed together as she hyperventilates, so I hold on to every word like a breath before going to the bottom of the pool.

"He fell..." Here it comes. "into a machine, Ella." Shit. Shit. Shit. You know how I said I almost never cry? Now this was an event where that went out the window. Through tears, I try to speak to her.

"Mom...mom, stop! I'll be home by noon."

When I got in the car, I was blind with tears. I spent 2 and a half hours with my parents and Duke before I had to make the three hour drive back to Seattle for an eight o'clock show. I have never cried so much in my life. The police had told us that, according to the security cameras at the mill, it was definitely an accident, which we sorta knew going in. What we didn't know was that we wouldn't even be able to bury him. There was nothing left. Nothing to mourn, nothing to love, nothing to say goodbye to. All they found was blood and clothes. I sincerely hope I don't die like that. Louis died without even a face to kiss goodnight for forever.

I guess it helped my emotions that I hadn't said a word to him in three years. If it weren't for Facebook, I wouldn't even know what his growing up had done for his looks. I cried until I got back to the apartment, then it turned off. Tears are my enemy. Enemies get in your way. I kill things that get in my way.

*****

When I returned to the theatre, I was in character. Stella Kowalski, not Ella Rose Buchanan. Deep breaths, I told myself. It'll all be over soon. My sister in Streetcar, Blanche DuBois, is played by one of the...girls (I shudder). She has aggravated me from day one of rehearsals. She's fine onstage, but offstage...well, you'll see.

As I enter the makeup room, four of the five chairs are occupied. Mia, playing Blanche, sits next to the only empty one. I sigh, taking my seat next to...it. "Ten minutes later than usual, Miss Buchanan. You get dumped or something?" She adds the last part as she sees my red rimmed eyes. I glance at her, shooting daggers through my retinas at her.

"Don't worry, you'll be able to be on bottom someday, just don't ask right away." She laughs and two other girls laugh as they overhear her crude humor.

I can feel the heat rising in my cheeks as their piercing hyena cackles make my hands ball into fists, and tears again begin to form in my bloodshot eyes for the thousandth time today. I don't say anything, and start to put on my makeup. But they won't...stop...laughing. My brother died today, and I bet the worst part of their day was missing a sale on the cutest shoes. The last thing I remember before it happened was shaking. To put the final cherry on this nuclear sundae, Jimmy pops his head in.

"10 minutes until the house is open!"

Mia chimes in, "Ya only need ten minutes, anyway, right, Ella?" Even Jimmy smiles at this sexual innuendo. And that's when I snap. I haven't even put mascara on before I stand up and begin to walk out, then I stop. What happened next wasn't probably the smartest move, looking back, but goddamn it felt good. The feeling of dieting for months and then finally eating cake and ice cream again, being single for a year and then having the best sex of your life during a one-night stand,

or even losing your voice for a week then getting it back when you sing in the shower.
I punched Mia the Bitch square in the face. Blood poured from her perfectly shaped nose as soon as I felt a crack under my knuckles.

Feelin' good.

She's so shocked, she doesn't react for a second. I'm so full of rage, I think my eyes filled with tears that streamed down my face before hers even began watering. She fell out of chair, and was helped up by Jimmy, as he rushed inside.

"Ella, what the fuck are you doing?!"

She doesn't even have time to look at me again before I kick her so hard (we'll say in her vaginal region, for lack of a more family friendly term), my Chuck Taylor's toe can actually be felt going inside her. She doubles over, and I'm about to leave when Jimmy grabs me by the shoulders, spit flying as he speaks.

"You get out of my theatre, Miss Buchanan. You're FIRED!"

I glare into his face, our noses exchanging sweat through contact, as I shout at him. "I'm glad. I've had doubts about you since Rent ended! You were never the same! You're beating a dead horse when you don't have the legs to kick it anymore! I hope you rot in hell, asshole!"

I slam the door on the way out of the theatre, crying so hard tears are hitting the ground and leaving a trail. Turning right, towards the apartment. After half a block, I slow my pace a fraction, and then I see him. A man, playing the tenor saxophone. That's what Louis plays. Used to play.

***

I lay on my couch for probably 20 hours, not knowing how to proceed. In one day, I had lost a job, assaulted a woman, alienated a director, probably forever, and my family had been torn apart. So I watched How I Met Your Mother. 2 seasons in one day. The first marathon I haven't enjoyed. 48 episodes and two entire party bags of chocolate covered pretzels later, I was feeling even shittier than when I started. Screaming into a pillow doesn't help, and nor does making myself vomit to make the unrest in my stomach go away. Hair pulled back, bent over the toilet, I hear a knock on the door. No, not a knock. A pounding. At 2...damn...AM.

When I open the door, I'm hit with the disgustingly sweet and almost foreign scent of alcohol like I've walked into a glass screen door without realizing it. The disheveled figure leaning on my door frame is, of course, the once great James Atwell.

"If you're gonna do anything but apologize, leave."

As he speaks, his breath makes me gag. "'Ella, if you're still interested in coming back to the show, we can make ourselves a little deal." Those words would stay with me forever.

He pushed through my door, sex the only thing on his inebriated mind. I don't remember the words after that, I just remember the actions. The shove onto my wood kitchen floor that would leave bruises for weeks. The sinking feeling as he collapsed onto me. The pressure on my arms as I tried to fight him, failing miserably. My scream, that probably did nothing but stir the cats upstairs. The pain of his aggression radiating through my stomach like a bomb. The tears once again streaming onto the floor, pooling next to my cheeks. The next eternity was agony, and then 10 minutes later, gasping for breath, he rose off of me, zipping his pants and smiling down at me.

"I'll take that as a no to that deal, then." He shouted something as he slammed my door, something that I wouldn't remember until the next day, after I had regained consciousness.

I woke up with his semen still inside me, with barely the energy to lift my naked body off the floor and shower the horridness away. I couldn't scrub enough to feel clean during the half hour long shower.

Want to know a secret?

That's how I lost my virginity.

I had never truly felt hate until that moment.

Blues

<u>Journal Entry 3: Blue Skies</u>

November 12th, 2012

Ella. Her name is Ella. I can't believe I actually spoke words to such a masterpiece. I just about thought I would never see her again. I even drew a picture of her while I still had her beauty locked in my endless mind. I wanted to at least be able to look at her if I never got to confront her or even see her occasionally walking into 5th Avenue. I thought that was the only chance I had to talk to her and she would be gone from my life forever, but I have been proven wrong. Not only that, but I get to see her again on the 18th and I couldn't feel any happier.

How did this happen exactly? I was playing outside of the 5th Avenue once more on a Saturday while waiting for Jimmy to finish directing his current show to just see if I could maybe see her again. I had done this for a couple of weeks and then came across today. Today was the day I formally met Ella. As I was playing Red, she tip-toed awkwardly up to me and placed money in my empty, tattered case. I immediately stopped playing and she looked startled. She stuttered a bit when speaking to me.

"Oh! Did I make the wrong move? Do you want more money? Why in the world did you quit playing?"

I chuckled and spoke "No, no, stop worrying. I just wanted to give you your money back. I'm not playing to receive anyone's money. I play to share my music. I could care less about money."

"If I'm being a grammar Nazi, it's 'I couldn't care less. But seriously? You don't want a single penny? I don't think I have ever met a man in Seattle who wouldn't take free money" she said surprised.

"Seriously." I said with a grin. I thought the

conversation was going to end there because she had began to slip away, but suddenly she turned back around and walked up to me again.

"I haven't heard someone play good jazz on the streets of Seattle since I moved here. It's nice to hear beautiful music while walking on the streets in the cold. You play just like my... you play wonderfully." I could barely think properly after hearing those words slip through those pristine lips.

"Thank you so much. It's really just something to keep my mind off things." Then, something happened that I never thought would.

"Well, I absolutely adore it. I'm Ella, by the way, what's your name?"

"I'm Quentin" I spoke, flattered.

"Quentin, eh? I think I'm going to call you Quint. Let's meet up for coffee and talk jazz." she said as she wrote down her number on my palm and slowly made her way to the closest Starbucks.

I've never been called "Quint" before and I sure damn hope it isn't that last time I get called that because she will be the only one to do so. I couldn't believe it. I can barely comprehend that she wants to see me again. I haven't had a day this invigorating in months, years even. This sentiment better sustain for amounts of time unimaginable to the human mind because the minute it slides carelessly away, both my mind and body take over one another and my existence is no longer reality.

***

Waking up to the grumbling sound of the garbage truck driving through the tightly packed alley-way between my studio apartment on 6th avenue and the building across from it that is ran by some sort of company, I assume, I realized that today was no ordinary, bland day. The sounds of banging and crashing didn't antagonize me as they tend to do every Tuesday morning. I didn't open my eyes disappointed at the fact that the flat I live in consists of a pile of unwashed clothes that I have been just about far too lethargic to take to the laundromat, endless cups of finished black coffee laying carelessly about, unrefined artwork that may never even be touched by a drawing utensil ever again, and at least one different instrument laying in any area one is to look. None of it mattered to me today because I have been waiting for this for about 1 week and I couldn't feel more exhilarated.

As I expeditiously pull the covers off of myself, take the glasses off my bedside table and put them on to actually be able to see, I spring out of bed and immediately place a random vinyl on the maroon, turntable near the top-right corner of my bed. Fever by Little Willie John begins to play as I slip into the kitchen to make my daily cup of black coffee along with toast that is just about to the point where it's a crispy texture, nearly black, but not entirely burnt.

"...When you kiss me, fever when you hold me tight, fever in the mornin', an' fever all through the night."

I begin gathering "Red" together in his raggedy, dark blue case before getting dressed. I slip on the first item on my rack, which happened to be a slightly tattered, forest green flannel, one of the three pairs of dark-blue jeans I own that all consist of at least one tiny rip, my oxfords, and an old, black bowler hat. Calling up Jimmy, I walk out the door to head down to Ground Zero.

After 3 buzzes, the phone is picked up.

"Hey man, what's up?" says Jimmy sounding slightly hungover.

"Hello, I'm about to head down to Ground Zero and was making sure you were on your way as well, so we can play some tunes, maybe even mix it up and try something new." I spoke in reply.

"Uh, yeah be there in a few." he says with slight evidence of panic tracing from his tone.

"You better be."

"I will, Quentin. See ya." said Jimmy with

frustration.

"Uh..Bye?" I say as getting practically cut off.

Putting my phone in the back pocket of my tattered, blue jeans I relentlessly walk to Ground Zero. The roads didn't seem as depressing this morning. The sounds of muttering engines, the murmur of the people walking next to one another on the sidewalk, the raggedy red-headed man playing his out of tune, beat-up acoustic guitar. None of that gave me the headache I tend to receive every morning on my walk to the coffee shop. It felt nice to not feel all the frustration my mind tends to give me every misty, Washington morning.

The last block of 6th avenue was coming to an end and directly at the corner lay the best coffee shop in all of Seattle (to me, anyways. It's way better than the typical Starbucks White Chocolate Frappuccino everyone loves so much, apparently). Carrying "Red" on my left shoulder, I walk in to an empty coffee house smelling of freshly roasted, ground-coffee beans and the sound of Ella Fitzgerald's sweetly toned voice playing faintly over the stereo that most employees plug their cells in to play music from Pandora. Located at the back of the shop is, what most like to call "The Bar", but they don't serve a single trace of alcohol in any of their scrumptious drinks. To the right is a small stage full of clutter because of the chords from the sound system, the Yamaha keyboard, and two microphones and mic stands set up for Jimmy and I. Around the red, brick walls of the place, white lights in the shape of latte mugs string about. This place didn't have the typical restaurant set-up of tables, chairs, booths. There is sets of old couches, love seats, and even bean-bag chairs. This place gives just about everyone who steps foot inside a warm feeling, as if you are walking into somewhere that is practically home.

It was 9:00 a.m. now, 30-45 minutes after my phone call to Jimmy, and he just scurried into Ground Zero, practically out of breath.

"Man, did you sprint here? It looks like you are struggling for a breath" I said as if I was worried, but I honestly couldn't care less about him at the moment.

"I'm so sorry, Quentin! I didn't mean to take this long! I had to finish up some Director business, the bus had already left, and I had no choice, but to run because I left my phone back up in my office." Jimmy spits out suddenly.

"It's whatever, Jim. I want to play, so put your trombone together and let's get started. I already have Red put together and he's ready to spew awesome tunes." I say with a chuckle under my breath.

Jimmy laughs and says "You never do get mad, do you Quentin?"

"I guess not" I lie.

Stepping on the small, cluttered stage, Jimmy follows behind with his trombone at his side (he refuses to name his instruments, which bothers the hell out of me, because he thinks it's pointless). Suddenly the world turns off for a moment. I place the mouthpiece of "Red" in my mouth slightly and close my eyes. These instants, the times in my life that I step on a stage, or simply playing on the streets of this crowded city on a Sunday afternoon, are something I completely cherish. I find myself pressing my finger tips down creating music more beautiful than ever because it's all me. I may play with a partner by my side, but once the match of music is lit, the flame will shine as one. I don't create the music I play, the music I play creates me. As the people slowly creep in, ordering drinks, talking quietly to one another, I barely even catch a glimpse of who is in the room. It's as if no one else exists, but "Red" and I. Then, the song will end. The song comes to an end and there are slight claps throughout the small coffee shop, smiles from corner to corner. That's the moment reality switches back on again and I see the faces of people shine after listening to something so incredibly moving. I smile to the crowd, I even slip in a wink from time to time, and start playing some more.

Novelette

Fresh air always helps, right? The long walks amidst the Seattle rain have cleaned out my heart and soul before, and they will do it again. God, I love rain. What a perfect way to take all the sludge and dirt from your insides and wash it out in seconds, where no one can distinguish the falling droplets out of the sky from the ones out of your eyes, and where everyone is an equal. Whether you're a billionaire or you're homeless. Everyone, no matter what, ends up wet.

Over the next several hours, I'm all over Seattle, trying to forget about the previous day. But everywhere I look, whether it be Pike Place Market, or Benaroya Hall, I see James Atwell, all business, acting as if nothing has happened. His face reflected at me in a store window, his broad stature forming an all too recognizable silhouette inside a passing bus, his voice, even two months later, after it happened. We can make ourselves a little deal. I shiver, not because of the cold.

Out of the corner of my eye, suddenly, I see the 20 foot tall flashing sign marking the 5th Avenue theatre, where Jimmy must be at this very second, just around the block from me. To even imagine that I am this close to him sickens me and I feel like vomiting. Swallowing, I clench my teeth as I break into a run toward the damn place, hoping to get one last spat word at him before I slam the door on him for good. I imagine strangling the bastard, killing him with my bare hands. My forearms cramp from how hard a hold my fingers around his throat. The surprise on his face slowly turn to rage, and then to horror as I suck the life out of him. I feel his pulse, so fast his heart may give out. What a coward, so scared of death. His eyes grow bloodshot as he begins to pass out, and he chokes on nothing. As his eyes roll back into his head, I still don't remove my locked hands. When I finally do let go, the only thing I can think to do is to leave his body out in the open to be found, cold, hours later, alone and afraid, just like I was the night he...

All of a sudden, I stop. I hear tenor saxophone again, just as I had yesterday. Within two measures, I recognize the song. Blue Skies, Ella Fitzgerald, for whom I was named. I know it's the same player. I haven't heard someone play tenor that well since...well, a while. My anger falls off me and onto the movement, the ceramic coating it encases me in shattering on the pavement so quickly and completely I even feel like singing along. Of course, my voice is absolutely destroyed from the crying yesterday, but it's the thought that counts, yes? He's across the street from the 5th, in the middle of a courtyard shadowed by the massive Rainier Tower. I don't bother to look both ways in my eagerness to cross the street towards the music. If a car had clipped me driving by, I'd bet I wouldn't have noticed. When my foot touches the opposite sidewalk, I couldn't have told you Jimmy's last name for all the money in the world, that's how focused I am on the sound. I'm searching all my pockets until I find a five dollar bill to give to the man...or boy. He looks somewhere in the middle. He looks twenty, but is probably older than me. Not sure how I can tell, but he gave off, even from thirty feet away, an aura of wisdom. Like safety.

I tip-toe up to him, feeling amazingly awkward, like I'm naked on a table, ready to be probed. I place the money quickly in his open case, and am taken aback by him. He's got a very unique face, that's for sure. Shrouded by a mess of dirty blonde hair, his eyes closed behind glasses with thick black rims. I wouldn't say I was attracted to the man, but he was attractive. He's stopped playing, I now realize. Now I'm just awkwardly staring at him, probably with my mouth gaping, drooling on the ground. Shit.

"Oh! Did I make the wrong move? Do you want more money? Why in the world did you quit playing?" I stutter on every other word, Jesus Christ. I don't understand why I seem to be intimidated by him, I just am. He smiles at me with slightly crooked teeth. Damn, that's attractive.

"No, no, stop worrying. I just wanted to give you your money back. I'm not playing to receive anyone's money. I play to share my music. I could care less about money."

Bold, I like that.

I remember uttering something about his incorrect word usage, then a comment about how it was odd that the man wouldn't take free money. Seriously?

"Seriously." He replies, running his fingers up and down the keys on his tenor.

"I haven't heard someone play good jazz on the streets of Seattle since I moved here. It's nice to hear beautiful music while walking on the streets in the cold. You play just like my... you play wonderfully." (he reminds me so much of my brother that I can't take it. Not that I find my brother attractive or anything.). He smiles even bigger, looking down at my feet, dimples forming in his cheeks.

"Thank you so much. It's really just something to keep my mind off things." Isn't it always? I introduce myself at this point, feeling awkward standing here for so long.

"Well, I absolutely adore it. I'm Ella, by the way, as in Fitzgerald. What's your name?"

"I'm...uh...Quentin." I love that name. That sounds like a name given to someone that would one day be a wonderful jazz artist.

"Quentin, eh? I think I'm going to call you Quint. Let's meet up for coffee and talk jazz." I give a guy my number for the first time in my life. What's gotten into me?!

Blues II

After playing 5 pieces or so, Jimmy and I usually stop to take a quick coffee break because we get drinks free for playing. I walk up to "The Bar" and tell the blonde, blue-eyed barista, who is on the job every time Jimmy and I play "Why don't you surprise me this time, Minny? I always order the same thing and I've decided to change it up a bit on this special day. Make it decaf though because I plan on having caffeine after 5 more songs."

Smiling she says "Anything for you, Quentin. What a wonderful job you guys did up there, as you do every time. It was nice to hear something new! Why is this day so special? I haven't seen you this happy in awhile."

"I met a girl. A very beautiful girl." I say as I feel my skin on the tip of my cheeks heat up.

"I'm so happy for you! Good luck today! Here's your coffee." She says with a huge grin upon her pale face.

I take a quick sip of the coffee forgetting the fact that it is super hot, burning the tip of my tongue "Ouch!" I squeal.

Minny says startled "Are you alright?"

I begin to laugh "Oh, no don't worry about me, I'm fine. I'm curious, what is it?"

"Coconut white mocha. What do you think?" she says in the tone just about every female barista speaks in when telling the customer about their drink.

"It's delicious, thank you!" I tell her as I walk over to the couch closest to the stage.

"You're welcome!" She yells to me as I walk away to sit with Jimmy.

It's was 10:32 a.m. and soon Ella would be meeting with me at the coffee shop and I couldn't be any more excited than I already am. She told me over the telephone that she would be here by noon and the clock seems to move slower than it ever has waiting for her to walk in. Will she walk in happy to see me? I surely hope so because I'm so delighted to see her.

***

We had played nearly 4 more pieces before a feeling of light entered the room and the music sounded far more engaging that it had ever been. I wasn't kidding when I had said that everyone in the crowd was an absolute blur, but something changed that. In the corner of my left eye, I spot her and even the tune begins to fade to the back of my mind. Everything around me freezes completely, but us. She wasn't dressed up, she didn't put any make up on to try and impress me in any way, her pale skin and flattering eyes just glowed more than anything in the room. I stopped playing to let out a huge smile.

Suddenly, everything began to move again and a tear slid down her right cheek as she stormed out of Ground Zero. A rush of confusion hit me in an instant and nothing that just happened made the slightest sense to my muddled mind. I just about drop "Red" on the edge of the stage, when setting him down so quickly, and bolt out the front door to try and catch her. Just like the first time I laid my eyes on her, I wanted to comfort her and find out what was wrong. I wanted to help her, make things better, and make her smile.

"Ella!" I scream down the block. She was nowhere to be seen. I walk around the corner of the alley and there she was. Her head in her knees as her bag lays beside her and she begins to shake.

I immediately get on my knees to be closer to her and speak softly "Ella, whatever I did in there, I didn't mean to hurt you in any way. Did I do something? What is wrong? I'll do anything to help"

She didn't say anything. She just continued sitting there as her knees were hugging her alluring face. I sit next to her for a few minutes and realize what I should have said. I start rubbing her back softly, telling her "I may know nothing but your name and how beautiful you are, El. However, seeing you hurt like this isn't something I want to see and I doubt you want to feel whatever it is you are feeling. Here's the thing, you don't have to tell me what happened in there, but I'm sure as hell not going to leave your side until I see that smile of yours. You will leave happy because a girl like you deserves to be happy more than anything."

She lifts her head up from her knees and says "Quint..."

"Ella, let's go on a walk. There's a park near us that is probably only a mile away. We can get coffee another time." I tell her, cutting off her words.

"I would like that." Ella says as she stands up.

Starting the walk to the park, the streets started to get busier, crowds started to grow slightly larger, and the noise grew louder, but we were silent. Not a word was spoken and I didn't mind that. Walking with her by my side made strolling through the city calming. It was as if she cut the string that caused all the restless noise in my mind.

After a mile or so, we had reached the park.". We walked in silence around the park once then same to a stop near one of the benches and sat down. Placing my arm around Ella, she looks at me saying "you haven't said a word this whole time, Quint".

"You didn't either." I said smiling.

"I really enjoyed it. I could figure out things in my head without feeling alone" Ella said.

I did nothing, but smile.

"Can I trust you?" she asks.

I look to her saying "Only if I can trust you".

We both start laughing and she stops to say "What happened at Ground Zero back there was practically a punch to the face. I want to be able to explain this whole situation to you. I just need to make sure I trust you enough to do so."

"What proof do you need other than my words?" I ask, giggling.

"Hmm.. stand up so I can get a good look at you.

I need to make sure you look the part." she says as I begin to lift myself off the bench, but she pushes me back down, laughing "Oh my god! I was completely kidding. I'm not that controlling. Nice to know you would do it to gain my trust though."

We chuckle together and I say "So, what did happen back there, El?".

A sigh released from her while she looked down at her old, beat-up Chuck Taylor's and spoke "I don't know where to start".

"Don't think about starting..." I said "just let your mind do the talking and start going with the flow."

"Okay, I'll try..." another sigh came out of her nearly chapped lips "...it was the man playing trombone up on the stage with you at the coffee shop."

Anxiously, I ask "Jimmy? Jimmy Atwell? What did he do to you?"

The minute she verbalized those words, my heart started beating much more rapidly than it ever has. I felt so cold inside because I always had this feeling about him. One day he was my best friend, my partner, but these past 6 weeks everything about him bothers me in some sort of way and I could never quite grasp on to the reasoning for it. It was hard for me to even process what in the world he could have done to Ella to make her hurt so badly. Without even knowing what happened yet, my hatred towards Jimmy was beginning to grow stronger than it ever has been. I felt like hitting something with all the strength there was inside of me. The rage within me has never been vigorous. As I felt myself heat up, I feel the touch of Ella's hand on my thigh.

"Quint?" she says, concerned.

"What the fuck did he do to hurt you, El?!" I yell as I press my fingers into my skull as a migraine starts to build up.

"Quint..." Ella repeats, petrified.

"I thought he was my fucking partner! I thought I trusted his ass. I don't even know what to think of him anymore and this just gives me more of a reason to completely turn on him. This past 6 weeks he hasn't done anything, but irritate the shit out of me and I don't understand why. I thought it was just me, so I thought I could let it go. I was gonna let it vanish as if it never fucking existed in the first place, but now I'm finding out he hurt you and without even knowing exactly what happened, I feel so much hatred towards him." I release and breathe.

We sit in silence for a couple of minutes as my throbbing head lays in my sweating palms, pounding as Ella sets her gaze away from me.

Ella looks back over to me and as if she is about to speak, but I jump in "El... I didn't mean... I... I'm sorry."

She sets her hand on my back, clearly showing she couldn't decide if rubbing my back was an okay thing to do, and utters "Don't be."

Here's the thing though, I am sorry. This was the first time truly hanging out and talking with this wonderful girl. Knowing myself, the slightest moves I make can screw up anything within an instant. If I leave this park today knowing I won't ever see her again, I'll feel completely empty. I have to do what it takes to make her happy, not scare the living shit out of her because my mind is going mad. I should have known better than that, after everything that took place back at Ground Zero. I'm an idiot, a complete fool. I took a couple more breaths and sat up correctly.

"Go on, El." I sigh.

"Are you sure?" Ella questions.

"Just speak. I won't say a word. I'll just listen. The minute I try to say something and you aren't finished, shut me up." I tell her firmly.

"Uh...Okay..." She mutters.

Pulling the hair out of her face, pushing it behind her ear, she begins to reveal what had happened with who was once my buddy, Jimmy Atwell.

"A couple of months ago my 22-year-old little brother, Louis, died" Ella let's out a sigh, refusing to let herself cry.

"El, I'm so sorry. What happened?" I ask.

"Just, shut up. You said you wouldn't say a word, so

don't..." she speaks with frustration. "... He was in an...accident. He was dead before he knew it and there was...nothing left." her breathing begins to pick up the pace.
"El..." I say under my breath. I had practically just met this girl and I find out about this and I couldn't feel so hurt. Seeing how much of a struggle it was for her to tell me this gave my chest and aching feeling. But, what in the hell did this have to do with Jimmy?
"You see, I've been in a show by the name of A Streetcar Named Desire as Stella and I had no way of visiting my family without missing a production. Your little partner, Mr. Atwell, is the current director of this show. For about 9 years now he has been my only director up until a few months ago after my brothers death. One of the cast members of this show thought it would be hilarious to make a pointless remark towards me about Louis as if it wouldn't hurt me in any way. I couldn't control myself. You don't just say rude things about a girls younger brother that died, ya know? My first instinct was to hit the bitch. I slammed my fist directly in her face without even thinking. I had never hit someone that hard before and it felt so good! And then I kicked her in her twat. And Jimmy saw the whole thing." she pauses and begins rubbing her eyes.

Nothing about her seemed sad. She was angry. She was so damn angry and I could see it in every aspect of her body. Her muscles trembling, her foot tapping uncontrollably, her voice weakening, and her fists tightly clenching as she begins pulling her hair. What in the fucking world did he do to this beautiful girl? She doesn't deserve this.

"They spent the rest of that performance as if nothing had happened, I assume, until that night. After seeing me beat that girl, he fired me on the spot. That was it. He had nothing else to say." she stops for a breath.

Was that all that happened? He cut her from the show and she is this hurt about it? Acting must mean a lot to this girl and judging from her reaction to just glancing at him, there's no way that was all that had taken place.

"The next day came around the corner in an instant..." she said nearly under her breath.

I knew it. I knew there was more to this story. I felt my stomach beginning to twist tighter and denser into a knot. A surgeon's knot, a lariat loop, or a hitching tie, maybe. It was as if I could throw up the McDonald's from yesterday afternoon right there, but at the same time it felt like one was pushing down on the food refusing to let it release.

"...Since I was kicked out of the show, I didn't show up to performances like I usually do just about every single day. Instead I sat around in my apartment watching How I Met Your Mother while scarfing down chocolate covered pretzels, but then a knock pounded on the door. I opened it up and there was Jimmy. He came over to apologize to me, but he didn't end there. He said to me 'Ella, if you're still interested in coming back to the show, we can make ourselves a little deal.' His voice was beginning to sound so seductive, alluring even. The only way I was allowed back was if I pleasured that son of a bitch. If I had sex with him right there on MY apartment floor and made that fucker happy..." Her voice got more intense by the second.

"I refused to let it happen, but he kept trying to place his lips against mine. He tried pulling my shirt off, pushing me towards him and I kept struggling and even tried screaming. That's when he stopped. He looked at me and said these exact words "Don't plan on seeing me ever again, Miss perfect" and he slammed the door on his way out. I couldn't help myself and immediately started to bawl and ever since that day, when I close my eyes I see his exact face as he said those damn words to me. He hurt me. Seeing him again allowed that to flash through my mind vividly just as it was starting to ease away. I hate that bastard. I fucking HATE him!" she started to yell as tears slid down those pale cheeks of hers.

I can tell she's leaving something out. I put my

arm around her softly, treating her as something so fragile, so astonishing. I will get some sort of vengeance on that asshole. I fucking *will.*

Novelette ii

Now I'm sitting on the ground at Gas Works Park park for a second time in two days with a guy I just met telling things I've never said to anyone. I really do wonder what's gotten into me. It's clear Quint is furious about Jimmy. I left out the truth, yet he is still absolutely, horribly, furious. I can see it in his eyes. If he knew about the...events...that truly transpired, he might kill someone.

Then the thought enters my head. Jimmy deserves to die. I know I couldn't do it. But maybe Quentin could, if I convinced him. How satisfying it'd be to watch his body twitch as the final pint of blood flooded from the cut in his throat...

Shit. I can't believe that thought came into my mind. But oh my god, I hate the man...

Maybe if you could make it look like an accident...

I can't believe I'm thinking this...

Quentin obviously likes me, I could probably convince him into doing some drastic...

That's crazy...

He could at least help me get the means to get back at Jimmy...

I can't. No no no no no...

I have to get out of here...

I have to leave...

I can't stay...

"Quint...I can't stay in Seattle. I have to leave."

A Spell

<u>Journal Entry 4</u>

November 13th, 2012

I could barely find myself falling asleep after yesterday afternoon. Just drifting into the thought of what had happened causes my palms to grow sweaty as my head aches in a pain so strong, the richest black coffee in the world can't even come close to comparing. It felt as if November 12th was a complete nightmare or a figment of my cruel imagination trying to blacken my heart.

Jimmy. James Leonardo Atwell has ruined everything from the start. I had plans for my future (well, for the most part). I wanted to go to art school and maybe have some of my pieces up in museums or other high-class buildings (anonymously, of course) while I played my sax as a hobby. He didn't like that. Jimmy wanted to partner up with me in hopes of becoming big, or famous even. Becoming famous is for ignorant, selfish, idiots who think they need other people to tell them they have talent just so they know they're "good enough". His plan didn't seem to work out so well being we play on street corners and coffee shops and haven't gotten any calls or suggestions (thank god). That wasn't it.

He injured El so terribly, every sliver of the event sinks deeper and deeper into my head as I continue to think about it. He tried to lay his revolting hands on her, and possibly more, as if she was some kind of mindless animal. He betrayed her in every way and I couldn't be more pissed about the whole damn thing. I may have just met this girl, but she was more than just a stranger after yesterday. It's as if she is my best friend. I don't ever want to lose her, and any idiotic lunatic that tries to hurt her deserves punishment.

What do I do about this? I can't just let this sit around and slowly rot like a pumpkin in December. I wanted that bastard to suffer. He deserved to sit in a sizzling, hot tub of his own remorse without having any way of escaping. I didn't want to simply confront the jerk. I wanted to hurt him with all the possible strength within me, but I can't do that because it may somehow upset El. I will do anything to keep myself from lacerating her feelings any more than Jimmy did. However, the problem with that is, I want that asshole killed.

***

Looking out my window, covered by the tattered, blood-red, almost crimson curtains my drunkie of a father had given to me for my place when I moved out of town (he gave me other pointless luxuries, but in all honesty, they don't matter), I kept contemplating whether or not I should try to contact Ella. I was afraid that, if I were to call or text her, she would simply think it was a little soon being I just saw her yesterday. However, I really wanted to speak with her. Sadly, I have a tendency to refuse doing things I really want to do because I have a fear of losing or screwing up on that matter or subject. I'm terrified of losing the friendship and bond I feel beginning to grow between El and I. It had just begun and I sure as hell don't want it ending anytime soon. So, do I call her or do I just sit here gazing at the pale, stray cat wandering and sniffing fearlessly around the half-empty garbage can searching for leftover chicken from neighbors down the hall?

I pull out my black, iPhone consisting of slight scratches and cracks from the endless times I have dropped the damn thing. Pressing "contacts" on the bottom right, I scroll a few spaces down and come across the contact named "El". My fingers start to quiver as I slowly move closer and closer towards the "call" button. I freeze and suddenly lose complete control of movement as my mind continuously instructs me to put the phone down. I rapidly lock it and place it in the back pocket of my slacks and slump my motionless body on my unmade bed. I wasn't able to do it. Maybe it was the fact that I was afraid to confess to Ella. I was petrified to tell her the truth because I didn't want her to think differently of me.

I pull out my weary, leather journal from my satchel and turn to the fourth journal entry and read aloud to myself "I want that asshole killed." I want the asshole killed. Two months ago I wouldn't have said these terrifying words or even write them down in a damn journal in the first place. What was happening to me? It was as if this "side" of me, Quentin George Harris (and yes, I know I have a terrible middle name), was no longer a side but a whole different person taking over my mind, holding it in their hands, and controlling it to mess with me. If that was the case, maybe I wouldn't seem so hysterical. Yet, what if there actually isn't anything wrong with having these thoughts and feelings? What if I'm one of the few "normal" ones on this earth and every other hopeless human being is crazy.

I hear my phone ring as I scramble around searching for it before realizing that I had placed it in my back pocket. It reads "El" and I immediately begin to panic and swipe to answer the call.

"Ella! I mean... El. Hi, El." Could I sound anymore deranged?

"Hey there, Quint. Uh, everything okay? You seem a bit nervous, anxious even." she says over a hidden giggle.

"Oh, don't worry about me. I just was in the middle of a project and I was startled." I lie.

"I'm sorry to interrupt. I can call you later if you like." she says happily.

"Oh, no, no... It's fine. I was just about wrapping it up for the day anyway. How are you, El?" I lie, again.

"I'm pretty alright. I just was calling to make sure I didn't come off too, well, straightforward and foolish." she speaks almost nervously, yet confident.

"What? No way! I totally understand that you were just super stressed out and there's nothing wrong with that. We all have to let out our hate and anger at some point, don't we?" I can't believe she thought she was the crazy one when I'm clearly going out of my mind.

"Oh, thank god. Thanks for understanding. I'll talk to you later?" Ella questions.

" Actually, I know the sounds kind of last minute and rushed, but would you mind meeting up today? I need someone to talk to. Jimmy was my only decent friend and he's now the last person I want to see." I can't believe I got the nerve to ask her. I was so damn scared a few minutes ago and now that I hear her voice, I'm calm. It's like she was the fire in the fireplace keeping me crispy and warm on a frigid, Seattle night.

"Of course. I'll be ready in about an hour. Meet me at the park? I'll bring Chinese food or something easy I can just order and pick up." she agrees to meeting up.

"That would be amazing, thank you." I smile while speaking into my cell.

"See you at 5, Quint"

"See you at the park, El" I hang up and place my phone back into my pocket.

After hanging up that phone, I began to grow anxious again. My heart started to race and my breathing was out of rhythm. I had to tell her. I must tell her about my feelings towards Jimmy because if I don't, I might just explode.

***

4:35 p.m. Only twenty-five minutes till I get to see Ella and I couldn't decide whether I was more neurotic or delighted about the whole thing. Gathering up my things, I check my phone for any new texts or missed calls. Nothing. I pull my satchel over my shoulder and exit my flat, locking the door behind me. As I approach the elevator, a sign that reads "do not entry" (Seriously? people really need to learn proper grammar because things like this irritate me so much). I pull out my phone a take a picture of the sign because this will definitely be even more hilarious days from now and why not have a funny story to tell Ella if things aren't going too well? On a dissatisfied note, the elevator being broken down meant I had to walk down several flights of stairs. It's not that I'm lazy, the staircase to these apartments are just absolutely frightening. The stairs creak and moan, water drips from the ceiling, and it echos due to the emptiness and brick walls.

When I eventually reach the bottom of the four flights of stairs, I stroll around to the back of the building and see my car. I wouldn't hate the damn thing so much if it wasn't a gift from my father who feels that gifts will make up for him neglecting me, on my 16th birthday. Although, it was the only car I had and with my salary, there was a very slight chance of me getting a new one anytime soon. It's a Chevy Nova, forest-green, with bits of the paint job chipping in random areas along the sides of the vehicle. I unlock the door and sit in the driver seat. It smelt of old people, cigarettes, and fake leather. I felt like I was sitting in my grandfather's car every single time I entered the thing. After turning the key a thousand times, well three times, the engine finally began to roar. 4:45. 15 minutes.

I stroll up to Gas Works Parks for the second time this week with Ella nowhere to be seen. However, she was running to get food, so it's completely understandable. After a few more minutes of waiting, I check my phone, 5:20 p.m. She's later than I would have expected, but I'm in no hurry. I gaze up from looking at the time and see El standing about twenty feet away holding a bag of Chinese food while she's looking around frantically. She was wearing a grey t-shirt with a title from some musical I didn't know existed and her messy, worn-out black high tops.

"El!!" I scream and wave to her smiling.

Ella slightly jogs toward me with a look of worry on her face.

"I'm so sorry about being 20 minutes late! The

traffic in this place is insane!" she says reaching for breath.

"It's no big deal." I say knowing how bad the traffic can get around here being Seattle is fourth place in the US for the worst traffic, right behind Honolulu, San Francisco, and Los Angeles.

We search to find the nearest bench and eat for a bit. We didn't say much to each other and I felt like it was my fault entirely. I kept thinking about what happened yesterday, barely speaking a single word. The hatred for Jimmy piled higher and higher in my brain every second. I'm trying too damn hard to keep myself from bursting into a million pieces in front of her. I don't want her to find me anymore of lunatic than she probably already thinks I am because of what had happened yesterday evening. I needed to tell her. There's only two outcomes to this situation. She either thinks I'm entirely psychotic or she understands me. The only way I'm going to find out is by telling her what is going on in my mind.

I must have grown red or my eyes were bloodshot because Ella looked at me and asked with her mouth half full "Quint, you okay?"

I nod a lie. I couldn't speak because I'm not fucking okay. I wanted the man that hurt the beautiful girl sitting beside me dead as he can possibly be. I can just imagine as he sobs from all the pain resulting from the slight slashes placed across his body randomly. The blood drooping out of him as I push him into a tub of gasoline, drowning that fucker and burning what is left of him. What am I doing? Ella is sitting right next to me and I'm plotting ways to kill Jimmy.

My mind is interrupted by Ella suddenly as she says "Quint...I can't stay in Seattle. I have to leave."

No, no, no. She can't leave. If she leaves, how will I get better? I need this girl.

"El, because of Jimmy? Please..." I say on the verge of tears from both the rage and the thought of her leaving.

"I have to" she says without seeming persuaded in

any way.

"You can't. El, I have something I need to tell you. You need to understand that you really can't leave Seattle." I say hoping she'll stay and listen to my words. I had to tell her now. I needed to persuade her to help me. If she leaves, I'll have no one, but myself. I can't lose her just as I lost Jimmy, my mother, or anyone.

"I have something to confess. I might seem absurd, deranged even. I'm absolutely terrified just thinking about the fact that I have no choice, but to tell you." I can't believe I'm doing it. "I...I..." I started to bawl. I felt completely idiotic to be crying in front of her.

"Quint, what is it? Trust me, you're not crazy." she says placing her hand on my shoulder.

I can barely speak now that I'm sobbing. I had no choice but to show her my journal. I had to show her what I wrote this morning if I can't speak it. I pull my journal out of my satchel, open it to page 4, and hand it to her as I quickly place my face back into my palms.

I look at her as she begins to read the passage and one single tear falls down her left cheek. "Something needs to be done, and I'm just not ready to be the one to do it." she speaks softly. As she gets up and walks away, toward who knows where, only one thought echoes across my brain.

Something needs to be done.

Waltz

I've always despised the 5th Avenue theatre, ever since I started rehearsals for Rent, just being inside the odd Americanized Chinese interior that I find so idiotic makes me frustrated. The feeling, now, is amplified tenfold. Just smelling what used to be where I spent most of my boring-except-for-performing day, makes me physically ill, sick to my stomach. The mob of people currently surrounding me makes it somewhat easier to forget. It's nice to actually be at a performance where I can mingle with the crowd and no one recognizes me (I wear a blonde wig in the show, and so much makeup that you can measure it by stepping on a scale.).

I feel extremely guilty about leaving Quint alone with his destructive emotions at Gas Works Park, but I had to leave. Running away turns out to be my best defense against my anxiety. It hits me so suddenly, with such raw ferocity, that if I stayed on the battlefield to fight back, I would likely end up dead. Today was no exception. Seeing the words he had written about Jimmy was terrifying to me. Not just because he was homicidal, but because we were both on the same page of this terrible novel called Hate. When I read those words, I want that asshole killed, I just exploded.

That thought had appeared in my mind as almost satire, an obscene overreaction to the whole event. Then this ape of a concept had stood up, knuckles dragging on the ground, evolving into something new: a possibility. Now, the neanderthal's back was becoming erect and upright as this possibility started to cross the threshold of reality.

Now I find myself here. At a Sunday matinee of A Streetcar Named Desire, without the slightest reason as to why.

I stay away from people, mostly. I enter the theatre, use the restroom (having to wait in line to relieve myself is the single most irritating feeling known to man, I swear...), and take my seat, the half an hour waiting period passing within seconds. I barely pay attention during the first and second acts, my understudy, one of the girls, doing an average job of filling my shoes. As soon as the fifteen minute intermission is signaled by the house lights blinding the crowd, I'm out of my seat. Something that I've forgotten to tell you...Jimmy, during the intermission of nearly every one of his shows, heads to the lobby to listen to people's conversations about his "masterpiece", which, more often than not, only serves to increase the size of his already enormous ego. I rush out of the theatre with a walk so fast I'm almost jogging. I catch sight of him instantly, with his back turned, the amount of product in his hair casting a slight glare onto the adjacent wall. I instantly memorize his outfit, so I can track him over the next fifteen minutes. Powder blue suit, black shirt underneath it, white and black leather shoes, hair with so much hairspray it could be a hat, and a tie to match the suit (Wow, he really sounds like a cattle auctioneer right now). As people start to flood the lobby, he turns, smiling at his "customers", until he sees me. His eyes flash with an emotion I can't quite identify and the shit eating grin drops from his face for a fraction of a beat. As soon as it disappears, it's there again, and he's chatting with a random couple about his work. Good to know I unnerve him.

Even standing fifty feet away from this monster, in the midst of an ocean of theatregoers, I feel my teeth clench uncontrollably, my hands in fists in the pocket of my jacket. I give it five minutes, so he begins to adjust to his surroundings and may start to slightly forget that I am waiting for him, on all sides, ready to pounce. I'm behind him now, as he's talking to a twenty-something who I assume is an aspiring actor or something. As soon as he bids her farewell, I'm on him, my hand casually on his shoulder, waiting for him to turn. His eyes widen instantly as our gazes meet, he has to look up, given that I'm a good inch and a half taller than him. That's a nice touch.

"Hi Ella..." he starts slowly.
"Shut up." I say quietly, tightening my grip on his shoulder, plastering a smile onto my face to avoid looking suspicious.
"Hey, Jimmy, I was just wondering..." I try to sound as casual as possible.
"...do you understand how much trouble you're in with me?" Still smiling. No response.
"Well, just to let you know, if I were you, I might find ways of protecting yourself." All my teeth still showing.
"Because soon, and I mean really soon, something's going to happen to you. And you will regret everything you've done in the past nine years. Talk to you later, Mr. Atwell. I'm really enjoying your show." As I walk out of the theatre towards home, I am no longer smiling.

Preacher Man

It's been days now, maybe 3 weeks even since I've had any sort of contact with Ella. After that day, it was as if she disappeared into some black hole deep in the midst of space. I tried contacting her by phone multiple times now and she has refused to return any of my calls or needy texts. I thought this would happen and I knew that if I were to try and tell her any of my vivid thoughts, I would immediately lose her. 3 lingering weeks have passed by and the same thing ran through my mind every minute.

Something needs to be done.

What needed to be done, El? I need to know because if these words don't escape from my atrocious imagination, I have no hope. She could have been talking about various things. Maybe she was on the same page as me and wants Jimmy killed or she possibly could have meant that she needed to leave Seattle like she wanted. I'm petrified when I think about the fact that Ella could no longer be any where near me. She may have left Seattle completely and if I have to wait another day, a week maybe, I might end up dead. I can't live like this anymore. I never thought words this simple would take over my body so quickly.

The ache surrounded me from the tips of my fingers to the heels of my shivering, bare feet. I haven't left my house or had contact with anyone since then. I was scared that if I were to leave, I would hurt someone or maybe even myself. I've been laying in the creaking bed before me watching reruns of *F.R.I.E.N.D.S.* hoping I would have the nerve to even eat something. I felt useless in this world consisting of pointless acts done by hopeless beings. There wasn't a point to anything anymore..I want to fall into a deep sleep, and I hope my physique refuses to gain life again.

***

Journal Entry 5
December 10th, 2012

Today is the day I have lost all hope. The day my body and mind have lost control and I can no longer handle such pain. What do I do now?

A. Try to contact El AGAIN.

B. Continue to lie here in my own thoughts as they begin to drown me out.

C. Forget about her and everything that happened in the first place, so I can move on. Start focusing on my art and music again, maybe find a job.

D. Confront Jimmy about everything.

E. Kill. Fucking Kill.

The correct answer is C, I know. However, the only thing that ran across my brain was E. Maybe it wouldn't be so bad after all.

***

Slamming my apartment door aggressively behind me, I take the first step, since the 13th, into the horrid, raining streets of Seattle. I will find that girl if it takes all the effort in the world and I mean that.

A homeless man is sitting on the street corner as I begin to turn on to 5th Avenue. Knowing my savings account was running a bit low, I hand him $10.00.

"Hey, man. Have a nice day, okay?" I say as I'm about to walk away.

A smile appears on the man's face as he says shakily "thank you, thank you, thank you, sir."

"It's really no problem. There's a coffee shop around the corner called Ground Zero. Tell the barista my name, Quentin Harris. Get something on me, alright?" I smile.

"Why? Why are you doing this?" he asks.

"Don't worry about it. Enjoy your day, man." I wink at him as I walk away slowly.

Damn. Was that even me back there?

Mazurka

It's been at least 2 weeks or more since I said those frightening words to Jimmy. Frightening for me to say them, frightening to think of saying them, and frightening to hear them, I'm sure. It wasn't the content that frightened, but what lay behind the syllables. I'm sure he heard, for it had been shooting through my eyes so clearly he would have to have been blind not to understand. I was going to hurt him. Neither of us knew how nor when, but both of us had a very clear idea of why. In these two weeks, I have not left the drab apartment, and the only two things on my oh so focused mind have been Jimmy and Quint. How to harm the former, and how to use the latter to do it.

I'm not sure what drives me to get out of bed, but there is definitely a hand on my shoulder this particular morning, pushing me onto my feet. The coffee tastes sweeter and bolder than usual, the bowl of cereal seems much more fulfilling than before, and when I look in the mirror, the horridly dark bags under my eyes from the past fifteen or so late nights and early mornings of nothing but wracking my brain have all but vanished from my face, and, after a two week non-stop rainstorm, the sky was clear, the sun saluting the many soldiers down below with a much needed 73 degree day, slight breeze between the buildings, spots of clouds here and there.

The thoughts on my mind until this beautiful morning have been as follows:
I want to kill James Atwell.
I want to make him feel the pain I felt.
Who am I kidding? When I'm wronged, I retaliate tenfold.
How do I kill James Atwell?

However, a morning such as this had changed my

thoughts:

I'm not going to kill James Atwell. I want to expose him. I want everyone to know what he did to me. It doesn't even matter if the son of a bitch is convicted, so long as people believe my words in print. Well, what do we need to expose someone? We need a journalist, and I'm going to find one.

First things first, I needed to get out of the apartment. As my feet touch the pavement, the sun's rays seem to hiss on my skin, foreign to the outdoors after two weeks of solitude, as if I was bacon on my mother's cast iron skillet. I begin walking in the general direction of the theatre, not because I want to see Jimmy again, but because I know my favorite saxophone player will be there, and I want him involved if I'm going to take action. Apparently that courtyard, across from the 5th Avenue, under the shadow of the Rainier Tower is our official "spot". He wants to see me, I know it, and that is where he'll be.

It just so happens that I am exactly spot on, as I round the corner, where a horde crowds around the box office to see the "final Seattle performance" of Streetcar, I hear a tenor saxophone, and it's belting my favorite tune.

Evenin'

I find myself carelessly wandering through the busy streets of Seattle on a sunny, Friday afternoon, saxophone held in my left hand, with sweat beading from my skin. I must have looked disastrous. I haven't been showering regularly, shaving is the last thing to come across my mind when feeling like this, and shit, I even forgot my glasses on my cluttery art shelf (I have a shelf above a small desk beside my bed that holds all my artsy crap and whatnot). My breath had to have smelt of rotten cheese, or something along those lines, and my hair was practically a jungle, the Amazon rainforest for god's sake. I can't believe the mess I have become over the course of a couple weeks. I'm disgusting for letting myself go and having such little care for anything.

My mind was fixed on finding that damn girl. The only thing on my mind, besides the thought of how revolting my appearance has been these past several weeks, was to discover that El didn't leave Seattle. To see her walking along the congested sidewalk, macchiato in her hand, wearing her Broadway T-shirt, her beat up sneakers, as she hums a lovely jazz song, is all I need right now. I will find her or maybe she'll even find me.

My body comes to a complete stop just a block away from Ground Zero. Setting my case on the ground, I open it shakily, and pull out sweet, fabulous "Red". Damn. I missed playing him. I didn't think I would miss it this bad until I placed my quivering fingertips on the keys and it hit me in an instant. I was too caught up in the idea that Ella was the only thing to make me feel somewhat better to realize that music, art even, is my outlet. These sublime things are used to distract me from the vivid scenes replaying nonstop in my mind. Closing my eyes, placing my mouth over the reed, I almost feel tears emerge. Pressing the keys down passionately now, I blow air through the beautiful instrument. A tune so elegant enters the air sweetly. Without a doubt in my mind, I could feel the stitches healing, and I no longer ached. I felt good. Hell, I was Feelin' Good.

My hips began to slightly sway as my right foot tapped to the beat of Nina Simone's masterpiece. I felt myself releasing my thoughts into the music, nothing but that. You would have to be nearly irrational to not be in love with this song. It does nothing, but make you fall in love. I remember hearing this tune the very first time playing about in Ground Zero and I immediately fell into my own world. I couldn't help but ask the barista the artist and title, then urgently rushing to my apartment to print sheet music.

As I just about get to the end of the chorus, a voice appears to my ear.

"...and I'm feeling good."

The voice was so quiet to me because I nearly hear nothing but the sound of my sax, "Red". Startled, I pull the mouthpiece hastily from my lips and look up. I found her. I can't believe I actually found her.

Mazurka ii

Quint smiles as I sing with his saxophone, and he hastily removes the instrument from his neck strap to run towards him. As he hugs me like a best friend, I hug him back. I actually enjoy the embrace until I realize that I hate hugs and pull away. Silly Ella.

"I've missed you, El."

He can't seem to stop smiling. It's nice to be smiled at. I can't remember a single time in the past weeks where I've received a genuine smile. I like the feeling. Either way, I avoid the comment and get straight to the point.

"Quentin, I have an idea. However, I'm gonna need your help. A lot of it, actually." he looks puzzled. "I need to start off by telling you something".

I tell Quint everything about that night, everything I left out the first time I struggled to talk about it with another human. How Jimmy took my virginity and left me naked on the floor, not knowing if I would ever be okay again. And how, weeks upon weeks later, I still hear his voice in my ear, his face in every window, as if he's following me, getting in the way of things. His face turns red when I finish, and his knuckles turn white in fists, but he doesn't say anything.

"I'm sorry I lied to you and...didn't tell you everything. It's not that I didn't trust you or anything. It's just..." I struggle for words. I know this isn't the reason his rage was bubbling over, but I still felt obligated to apologize for keeping him in the dark. "...I didn't want you to react, ya know...stupidly."

This gets a tiny smile out of him, his mouth curling at one corner, and a miniscule dimple grinning at me.

"I don't wanna hurt him, Quint." he looks up from the ground. "At least not physically."

He nods. "How?" his eyes ask me.

"I want to get the story out there, like a virus, I

want people to know every fucking detail. And I want people to hate him for it."

"I like it", he says softly, sounding like his teeth are still clenched behind his quivering lip.

"However, I'm not a writer, and I'm guessing you aren't either. So...you can probably see where this is going. I need someone to write about my story and make it go absolutely viral. Can you hook me up?"

He nods once more. Again, there's nothing like teamwork.

Evenin ii

I find it hard to believe El doesn't want to lay a hand on Jimmy. There is no damn way all she wants is to expose that son of a bitch. However, I needed to help her. I have hardly been surviving without her uplifting presence.

My mind being completely frazzled from all the anger knowing the complete truth of what Jimmy had done to El, I think to myself "who could I possibly know that writes? Who could get the word out there?". Then, something clicked in the back of my brain in an instant. Minny. Minny from Ground Zero, of course! She was talking to me a month or so ago and I may be wrong, but I swear she said something about becoming a much more successful journalist than she had expected and thought about taking a break from being a barista, or something like that (it obviously wasn't that straightforward, but that's what I recall).

I pull out my phone from pocket, looking at recent messages to see if I had texted her recently, but I hadn't. All that was to be seen in my inbox was endless texts to El that I had sent over the course of 3 or so weeks. I can't believe I was that pathetic. Out of the corner of my eye, I find Ella glancing at my phone to see what in the hell I was up to.

"What's...uh..." she says as I immediately cut her off.

"Oh! I'm trying to find a girls contact on my cell. I know this barista at Ground Zero who may be a journalist. I'm not quite sure if I'm entirely correct, but for the most part, I think she is." I say quickly, avoiding the topic of all those idiotic messages.

"I meant..." I bring her words to a stop as she tries to speak.

"Her names Minny. Hopefully she'll be willing to help us out. She's not the most calming girl, but she's...uh... decent? And she's probably better at writing than she is at flirting, I'm sure" I chuckle as I speak.

She stops trying and giggles a bit at what I had said.

"Call her, text her, do something. You have no idea how bad I want this." she speaks urgently.

"Of course, of course" I say and scroll through few contacts until reaching "Minny" and begin entering my message to her. "Hey, Minny. It's Quentin Harris, the sax player from Ground Zero. My friend and I are in desperate need of a journalist who is willing to write for us, get a story out there, ya know? I remember you saying something about journalism, so if I'm correct, get back to me A.S.A.P." I type with the tips of my thumbs pressing against the phone, quickly.

"What do we do now, Quint? Wait?" Ella asks, almost frustrated.

"I'm sure she'll get back to us soon. She usually texts back quite fast from what I remember." I smile.

"Let's hope so. I'm not the most patient person, if you didn't notice" she laughs slightly.

"Oh, no, no. Trust me, you're not the only one" I let out a grin.

After 30 minutes or so of casual conversations, my phone buzzes, allowing my leg to jump. I unlock my cell and see a text that reads "Currently searching for a story to do a project my boss gave to me, so that would be wonderful. I'm practically free anytime. When would you like to meet up and discuss details?".

"Is it Minny?" Ella asks demandingly.

"Yeah. She's gonna help us out. What time do you want to meet up with her? She's free whenever." I tell her as her shoulders lose stress.

"Now" Ella asserts.

I begin typing in reply to Minny "Now".

Mazurka iii

While Ground Zero wasn't exactly the most official location to have a meeting, it was the easiest solution to a quick problem. Both Quentin and I order a plain black coffee upon arrival, and we take our seats near the back of the coffee house, awaiting the journalist. Minny was, to put it quite simply, a girl. Blonde haired, blue eyed, everything I had grown to hate as of recently. However, I tried to avoid a snap judgment, for she could be our only chance at getting my story out there quickly. She's wearing jeans and a t-shirt when she walks in (my kind of style, that certainly helps her case).

When she sees, she instantly smiles at Quentin, her eyes flirting with him from across the room, and she walks over, her hips swaggering from side to side as if she thinks she's some sort of supermodel walking down the runway. As she sits down with us, her preppy sounding voice makes my skin crawl. "So, I hear you've got a story for me. My name's Minny, by the way." She shakes my hand and is taken aback by my firm shake.

"We do indeed." I respond, satisfied that my handshake caused her pain. "Okay, Minny, I need you to promise me that you won't tell anyone anything about me without my permission. This has to be a secret until the right moment, okay?" She nods in response, and I begin to tell my story, from start to finish.

I begin with my high school graduation, the first time I met Jimmy, almost nine years ago. I go on to talk about King, the failed murder mystery, how I had to work at this very business until more work came along, how Jimmy cast me in Streetcar, the death of my brother, getting fired from the show (I gloss over the fact that I assaulted a co-star. That probably wouldn't make a very good sympathy story.), and, finally, how Jimmy...ya know.

Eyes wide, Minny has been jotting down notes on her phone as I go on for the past five minutes or so, and now she looks up at me, eyebrows raised.

"So...he fired you and proceeded to come to your home and try and convince you to have sex with him to get back in the show?" I nod.

"And...you want me to write this?" She sounds excited. Probably better than writing reviews for sandwich joints or whatever twenty-something journalists do. I nod once again.

"I'd be extremely interested." she says, as if I don't know my story's intriguing. "I'll get to work on a draft, and I'll check up with you for specific details." I hand her a napkin with my number on it (how cliche), and she's off immediately. I glance at Quentin.

"Well, that was a hell of a lot easier than I thought it would be."

Evenin' iii

As Minny walks out the door of Ground Zero, Ella and I make eye contact as she tells me "Quint, we need to make sure Jimmy isn't aware of this. I don't want him to suspect a single thing."

I immediately knew what that had meant. I had to meet up with the bastard, so he doesn't think I've gone insane or something. If I don't meet up with him, he may think I'm on the verge of doing something I shouldn't. I look back at Ella.

"I... Fine. I'll meet up with him to, I don't know, discuss our next piece while getting a drink from Ground Zero." I can't believe I agreed to do that. The thought of me coming into contact with him causes my stomach to twist and my brain to scatter tremendously. I didn't want to do it, but I had to because I didn't have a damn choice. I want to help El as much as possible and I will.

Saying my goodbyes to Ella, I walk out of the coffee shop and head home. I can't believe I'm doing this.

***

Almost unable to pry my body out from under the covers the next morning, I grab my phone off the cluttered coffee table and search for Jimmy's contact. I find it hard to grasp onto the fact I still have it when I don't want to see him in person or even text the man ever again. The difficult thing was, I didn't have a choice. It's almost as if I was being held by a piece of string that Ella is holding and if I make one mistake, she'll cut it and her existence will fade away.

I open a new message to be sent to Jimmy, and typed "Hey, man! Let's get together and have coffee this morning. I haven't seen ya in awhile and it would be nice to talk music at Ground Zero. Be there at 10:00 a.m.". I slam my cell on my bed intrusively and feel absolutely nauseated by the words I had just sent to that sick asshole.

My phone buzzes and the message reads "of course, buddy! See you there!".

I hate him.

After doing my normal morning routine, I head out the door leaving "Red" on my bed knowing I wouldn't need to play today. As I walk towards Ground Zero, I feel my heart rate beginning to speed up uncontrollably and my chest starts to throb. When I enter the coffee shop, it was practically empty from left to right. Not a single person was sitting on any of the furniture and behind "The Bar" was the barista listening to Evenin' by Hugh Laurie, assuming it was playing from Pandora. Jimmy was nowhere to be seen, so I had no choice but to wait.

After several minutes of counting inanimate objects around the room to keep my mind off the whole situation, Jimmy walks in all business, looking as if he was the king of the entire world. I check my phone to see the time. 10:36 a.m. That bastard's late.

Mazurka iv

On my way to Minny's apartment to give her more details (as per her request), the sun starts to disappear behind Washingtonian storm clouds, the rays of UV assassinated by a black mask, casting the entire city into shadow. I swear as I feel raindrops falling on my arms and face and step under a veranda to try and escape it, at least for a few minutes. Checking my phone to verify Minny's address, I realize that I'm actually fairly close to her apartments. Junction 47, as it's known, is only about 8 blocks away so, if I walk at a brisk pace through the rain, I won't be completely soaked by the time I get there.

Fighting my way through seas of hurried Seattle residents attempting to get out of the storm, I arrive at the base of her building within a short ten minutes and am buzzed in immediately. Water pours from my jacket as I step inside, the floor collecting water spreading in a puddle around my feet. I take the stairs instead of the elevator, being she only lives on the fourth floor. The halls are empty, and only silence greets me as I reach her door and, when I knock, I hear nothing from inside. Not shoes rising to answer my knocks or a voice that shouts "Come in!" There is nothing but silence. After thirty seconds, I knock again, louder, more urgently. She must be asleep.

I turn the knob just in case, and it swings open, absolutely, definitely, unlocked. As I step into the small apartment, hardwood floorboards creaking slightly underneath my feet, there is still nothing but silence to tell me hello. Walking around a marble counter into the kitchen, a slip and catch myself on a cutting surface. As I look down, a streak of blood sticks to my shoe, a trail of breadcrumbs leading to the "x marks the spot" at the end of a black rainbow. A dead girl lies on her own floor, face down in her own blood.

My feet slip as I sprint out of the apartment, my heart in my throat, slamming the apartment door behind me. Quint picks up almost immediately as I call him.

Evenin' iv

As many pointless conversations consisting of lies and more lies took place, my phone rings from my back pocket. Realizing it was El, I answer it. I immediately rush out Ground Zero as my head nearly begins to explode.

It wasn't good news.

Part Two: Chaconne

Ballade

In the weeks following Minny's death, Quentin and I have been basically inseparable. The fact that Minnie had died the very day we hired her to write about me is completely terrifying. After calling Quentin, I had called the police, which were on the scene in minutes, their boots banging loudly on the floor, past my hyperventilating figure and into the bloodied apartment.

I wasn't a suspect, I knew it. The cameras monitoring the hallway showed me walking into Minny's place and immediately walking out, and it was Minny that buzzed me into the building. So the murder must have taken place between when I entered the building and when I got to the apartment. However, there was no one in the hallway during that period of time, so the murderer must have entered and exited from the room's window. No prints, additionally, could be found, except for Minny's. Which left the police without a lead from the start. There was no evidence anyone had been in the apartment other than the fact that the victim had been stabbed in the throat and there was no murder weapon found within the trash cans and dumpsters within a mile of the location.

Someone is a step ahead of us, they definitely know what they're doing, and they are not fucking around. This person, the murderer at least, could not have been Jimmy, for he was at Ground Zero for the half hour prior to my visit to Junction 47. The flavors of being horrified as well as feeling frustrated combine to make a cocktail that makes me a mean, nauseated, drunk.

Even with my uncertainty as to who killed the girl, my position on Jimmy remains constant. I want him dead and, ya know what? He was involved with her murder. I don't know how he found out about us, and I know he didn't personally slit her throat, but he was a contributor. I have no proof, but I can feel it.

All of this epiphany and catharsis, however, is completely irrelevant if I can't first meet my own needs. It's been weeks since I've made a single dollar, and if I can't pay my rent and buy food, I will become not only a homeless singer starving to death, but I will be a homeless singer starving to death that doesn't care about being homeless and starving to death because all she wants is revenge. Know what happens then? I die, without a concern in the world other than the fact that Jimmy Atwell walks the Earth.

I'm a thirsty and minute creature, partially buried in a beach's sand. As a towering wave rolls towards me, I have two choices.

Run for my life to avoid being buried alive under a thousand pounds of water crush me, but I will remain thirsty without the water to quench my own exclusive drought.

Run towards the wave, towards my crushing fate, towards wonderful torrents of water that will prevent my thirst from overtaking my world, and replace the thirst with a black end.

If I get a job sufficient for paying my rent, I will be fine, but it will effectively end the chase for Jimmy. I can't just up and get a job, and still try tracking my enemy, I just wouldn't have enough time in the day, let alone a necessary abundance of time to discuss things with Quentin. On the other hand, If I continue my personal manhunt with the saxophonist at my side, I become homeless, starve, die, and so on. The first option, at least for now, appears most logical. Thus, here I am, once again in Ground Zero, applying for the second time for a job.

With Minny gone (Let her blue-eyed, American soul rest in peace, I feel obligated to add), the coffee shop on 6th was officially hiring.

"I'm telling you, I have the experience, people love to talk to me, and I love to talk to people (Haha!)." I lecture Linus, the owner of Ground Zero. Personality-wise, he's very easy to be around. He will let you drive the conversation how you want it, and he never ceases to compliment me on my looks, even though I know I look dreadful.

"Dude, I get that," Yes, he said the word dude. Welcome to Washington. "but I just feel like we might want to give someone else a chance."

Sounding like a kindergarten teacher with that last remark, I know Linus wants to be wooed into giving the "You're hired!".

"Okay, boss. I'll make this short and sweet. I'll sing for free when no one's playing, I'll work absolutely any hours you give me, even if it's midnight and you have one customer, and you don't need to give me holiday bonuses." This gets him to smile.

Needless to say, I got the yes.

***

"...and never again...I'll go sailin'!"

As Beyond the Sea finishes up, and four hands applaud me, the door opens and closes, boosting my number of audience members by fifty percent. I smile at Quint, expecting him to run up and hug me like usual. However, not even my smile is returned. As I signal to my co worker, Becky, that I'll be taking a short break, Quint and I take a seat at a table parallel and adjacent to the window. He doesn't speak, or even make eye contact, for that matter. Looking around to make sure we're not being watched, he slides his hardback journal across the table to me.

"Back of the last page." he tells me simply.

As I turn the pages, I see my name too many times to count. When I finally reach the correct one, all I see is a list of directions, almost like ingredients, titled Ricin. I don't recognize about seventy-five percent of the words on the list, and I stare at Quint blankly, searching his eyes for an explanation.

"We're probably on the same page when we think that exposing Jimmy is no longer a good idea, after...ya know." he utters the first cohesive sentence of our encounter.

"So...what is this?"

"This," he says, gesturing to the list, "is plan B."

Dream

Life no longer makes as much sense as it used to. Everything that has been happening throughout these past couple of months seem to be piling on top of one another, like the bundle of records sitting on the shelf above my turntable. Layers of dust between each vinyl consisting of beautiful music. The events taking place in my life currently are so graphic and vigorous. Whereas the positivity I had once had is slowly being taken over by the distasteful grime.

2 or so weeks ago, a woman I knew passed. This girl wasn't the most delightful person to be around. She wasn't different, unique even. She was nothing but one of the typical mistresses of Seattle, Washington who sip their cups of white-chocolate mochas, read Vogue magazines, and flaunt over getting their nails done and eyebrows waxed. However, I knew her, as an acquaintance of course, but she was closer to maybe even being a friend of mine. I remember when Jimmy and I would being playing our weekly tune, on a Tuesday, at the coffee shop on the corner of 6th Avenue and Virginia st. by Dimitriou's Jazz Alley, Minny would make us our regular and compliment us on our work with that cheesy smile of hers. Although she wasn't that special to me, I looked forward to her smile as she would tell Jimmy and I "great job!" while she handed us our drinks.

The only other time I knew someone that had died was 16 years ago (saying that makes me feel old, gross). November 16th, 1996 was the day my mother, Olivia Harris, passed away (be prepared to grab some tissues). However, it wasn't sudden like this was. I didn't receive some sort of phone call full of panic about the death. She had been suffering from ovarian cancer for 2 years, on and off. In case you haven't the slightest clue what that is, ovarian cancer is a decently rare cancer that takes places in women's ovaries. I remember finding out around the age of 12, sobbing, and squealing because the last thing I wanted was to have my mother die, but when it finally became her time, it wasn't so bad after all. Knowing how long she had been suffering this traumatic disease, I wanted her to be at peace and it was all kind of beautiful when I was saying my very last "I love you's" to my mother as she held my hand in the hospital that smelt of latex and cleaning supplies.

Unlike my mother's death, this situation was far more sickening. My mother got to die so peacefully as family members surrounded her and she told them how much she loved them with hardly enough volume that only few could actually comprehend what she was saying. On a positive note, she got her goodbyes, but did Minny? No. Minny must have been killed within an instant. I bet she could hardly even get one syllable to fall from her screaming mouth. Minny didn't deserve this cruelty. Jimmy fucking Atwell did. He deserved to suffer a lethargic, tedious death without a single goodbye. I want him to have no choice, but to be completely silent while his soul disintegrates into complete emptiness.

Something needs to be done and it is now time for that something to no longer be a need, but a will.

***

Journal Entry 6

Ricin

1. *Purchase Castor beans.*
2. *Boil beans on stove on high to soften the outer coat.*
3. *Remove the outer shell.*
4. *Cook the beans for about 10 more minutes.*
5. *Mash the beans.*
6. *Filter them.*
7. *Add solvent to mashed/filtered beans.*
8. *Extract the pulp from the leftover oil of the beans.*

***

Meeting up with Ella at Ground Zero ended differently than I had thought it would. Showing her the list I had made in my journal, I thought she would have have shown nothing but confusion in her devious eyes. Instead, the vibe she gave off happened to be curiosity, interest, and agreement. There was no antagonism between the two of us and the idea of poisoning the evil bastard that has done nothing, but cause pointless problems, was the one thing we both thoroughly agreed on.

Now, Ella lies on my once empty bed contemplating what plan seems most secure in order for this to work. I can't accept the fact that she was here with me and on the same page as I was. It was so cute to see her rolling spontaneously all over my bed when she couldn't quite figure something out, and the sudden "yes, yes, yes!" or "this is perfect!" pour out of her cheesy grin when something clicked in the back of her mind. Suddenly, Ella lets out a huge sigh of relief and slumps into the dip of my mattress as I'm sitting on the ground, piles of jumbled up papers and broken pencils beside me, planning out the recipe in better depth.

I let out a laugh when glancing at her "what's the story, Morry?"

Seeing the judgmental look in Ella's eyes as she laughs, she says "I got the plan. It's perfect. You just wait!"

"Well... kinda gonna need the plan, so I'm aware of the situation" I grin.

Ella begins rolling her eyes as she says "Smartass! I meant that you just wait for it to actually happen."

"I know exactly what you meant, El. What's the plan?" I ask as I feel the thrill building up inside me.

Ella hands me her notebook and it reads:

Plan B
Make the Ricin with Quint.
Store it in a used coffee cup from Ground Zero.
Have Quint call/text Jimmy to meet up at Ground Zero a.s.a.p.
While on the job, have Quint hand me the cup of Ricin as if it was an empty cup asking me to throw it away.
When Jimmy and Quint order their drinks, make sure to mix ricin in Jimmy's.
Jimmy drinks poisoned drink and BOOM!

Reading this brought a smile to my face because she is absolutely perfect. I felt like two nine-year-olds boys planning out how to beat the level they've been stuck on for days on a video game. When reading her words, she didn't seem terrified about anything. It all seemed so simple and easy as if this was all some sort of virtual world.

I break out a smile "I love... I love it, El." Did I almost just tell her what I think I was going to tell her? No, no no no no. I can't love her. That will ruin everything.

"I'm pretty damn proud. Let's make the stuff tonight and be ready by tomorrow. I'm ready to get this done." she asserts, confidently.

"Alright, alright. I'll grab all the ingredients I bought this past week and will get things started." I agree.

"Let's go!" showing most of her teeth, she makes a fist and pulls it towards her as if she was telling herself she did a good job.

I spring up off the chaotic piles of paper and stroll towards the kitchen. About a week ago, without letting Ella know a single thing, I bought all the products I would need to go through with this plan. Searching through the cupboards I come across the brown bag with all the items needed to do so. Pulling out the pot from the bag, I fill it halfway with water, then place it on the stove. Turning the oven on "High", I hear a shout from

Ella in my bedroom.

"How's it going in there Quint?"

Walking back there to see what she was up to, I tell her "pretty alright" and smile.

"Can I crash here tonight? I'm already here and I honestly don't feel like driving right now." Ella asks as she lets out a yawn.

Words spew out of me without hesitation "Yes, of course!".

I can't believe she want to stay here with me.

"I'll sleep in the living room out on the couch and you can have my bed."

Jesus, listen to me. It's like I do this for a living.

"Make yourself at home and holler at me if ya need anything"

Who am I?

She nods in response "thank you! I'm gonna head to bed. Goodnight, Quint."

"Goodnight, El. I lo... uh... sleep well." I almost did it again as i switch the light off behind me. Quint, you need to remember she is NOT your girlfriend.

I walk back into the kitchen with nothing but Ella on my mind. The water now boiling, I grab the castor beans out from the bag and place them in the pot.

This is actually happening.

***

Waking up the next morning, the back of my neck aches from the amount of time i had been laying on my garage sale couch that was, honestly, probably $10. The clock in my packed living room reads 7:08 a.m. I walk to my bedroom to check on Ella, slightly opening the door so one eye can peep through. She's still asleep. I pull out my phone and text Jimmy "let's play at Ground Zero today. Be there at 10, as usual."

I walk entirely into my bedroom to see a bra lying on the right side of my bed and a beautiful girl, lying there, one leg out of the covers and her mouth nearly wide open. Crawling onto the bed, I begin to slightly shake her fragile body and the only response I get is a tiny groan as she turns to the other side, facing me. Her skin was pale, yet so intriguing. She looked so incredibly peaceful. I feel myself leaning towards her alluring, pink lips as if I wanted to kiss her.

"What are you doing?!" Ella begins stretching as she opens her sleeping eyes.

My body flies off the edge of the bed and Ella begins laughing uncontrollably.

She pulls her head slightly off the edge looking down at me "you're dumb" she says with a slight laugh tracing behind.

I look at her as my smile turns completely upside down.

"Today's the day, El."

Ballade ii

The long walk from Quint's apartment to Ground Zero, fourteen or so blocks away seems more like a hundred. My hands shake as if I'm having a seizure the whole way there, Quentin always walking three blocks or so behind me so no one spots us together. He's already called Jimmy for a jam session at the coffee shop in ten minutes, so when we arrive, there's only seconds until Jimmy is sure to arrive.

Just so I'm not immediately recognized, my makeup is thick, disguising every natural flaw and adding new ones. My hair is pulled back into a bun and hidden under a beanie so I can't be identified by my trademark shoulder length chocolate style. Today, I dressed like a girl. Boots, a north face, and designer jeans my mom got me for high school that I somehow still fit in, makes me feel like I don't belong in my own skin, and hopefully, it's been long enough that this disguise will fool Jimmy long enough for me to do my job.

I wave to Linus when I walk in and he nods in my direction, helping a new barista to make a complex tiramisu latte. As I step behind the counter, apron on and hands washed, Quentin steps through the door, avoiding eye contact with me, so we're not identified as a pair. Becky cheerily compliments me on my outfit as she comes out of the bathroom. Of course she likes it.

The tension between me and the rest of the world is palpable as the wait until Jimmy's arrival counts down.

He's almost here.

What if he recognizes me?

What if I don't do this right?

He's almost...

As he struts through the door, all business, the hair on my arms stands straight out, goosebumps covering my entire body. Quentin smiles at him, and I can see the effort it takes. The bastard glances around the coffee shop, not settling on any one particular spot or person. Good sign. The two guys hug and start chatting loudly enough that I can hear their voices but not their conversation. God, this is nerve wracking.

Quentin nods to Jimmy and walks towards me quickly to proceed with the plan. As he hands me the coffee cup full of poison, he winks.

"Ready, El? Would you mind throwing this away for me?"

I nod and smile like a girl. "Sure, buddy."

With the coffee cup in my hand, I cross behind the counter and place it behind the bottles of syrup so my co workers won't easily notice it. The couple minutes between then and when Jimmy strolls over to the bar to order a free drink pass slowly, as if the batteries in the clock are about to die and it takes the second hand five minutes to display thirty seconds.

"Hey, Becky. Would you mind surprising me today? That seems to be what Quint's been doing, and I figured, ya know, why not?" I overhear as he chats up the other girl on my shift. Oh, I'll surprise him.

She smiles at him then glances at me, the smile leaving her face as she drops character for a second. "Ella, use your best judgment."

I nod, grinning. "Alright!" I raise my voice so Jimmy doesn't recall what I sound like. I begin making my personal favorite drink, a coconut white chocolate mocha. Since it's likely this is the last drink Jimmy will ever have, I least make it well. If you're to do something, do it right. I get more nervous with each pump of white chocolate, each dash of coconut. I'm actually about to do this. As I finish the drink, I walk quickly over to the bottles of syrup where I hid the coffee cup with the ricin. Making sure I'm not being tracked, I remove the lids of the cups and pour the locha into the poisoned cup, throwing the original cup into the trash swiftly and quietly. After stirring the mixture so the ricin is evenly distributed, I hand the drink to my barista.

"This is that coconut white mocha for the trombone player." I tell her, nodding at Jimmy, playing trombone on the stage. "I'm gonna run to the bathroom really quick, cover me." She smiles and nods.

As I stroll to the bathroom, I imagine Jimmy Atwell dying. The tears pooling in his eyes from the abdominal pain that won't let him get a wink of sleep tomorrow night, followed shortly by hours in the bathroom, vomiting to the point of dehydration. He thinks it's simple food poisoning until the next day, as his sides split with agony and he finally dies alone, afraid, and without a chance of making it out alive. Just like Louis had died. With no one to hold his hand.

Bang Bang

Taking a sip of french roast black coffee, sun shining through the curtains beside me, as I find myself finishing up a drawing I was working on of a clarinet on fire (I call it Clarinet On Fire), my fingers shake repeatedly while placing the pencil tip to the sketch paper. The nerves in my body were doing nothing but buzzing as I thought about the actions performed a couple days ago. However, I didn't feel a single trace of satisfaction or fulfillment from what we had done. It felt like James Atwell, all business, was still on this planet walking over all of us, with his shit-eating grin, while pretending to be so kind, but he was purely, without a doubt in my mind, a man one would see hugging someone, smiling, while stabbing a stiletto into someone's spine. I could feel rage building up within my brittle body as more and more thoughts jumbled over one another.

While I take several breaths, soothing and cooling myself down, I take into consideration that Ella is just a room away. Laying her pale, immaculate body on my wrinkled sheets, drinking my coffee while listening to my music play from my turntable, and staying by my side through all the pandemonium in this world. I'm astounded by the fact she hasn't ran away back to her lovely all-about-jazz family, or tried to get back on track with her own life. Instead, she decided to stay in this hell with me and suffer from whatever I'm dealing with right now.

Not only did the thought of such a breathtakingly flawless girl, laying on white-sheeted bed, causes me to question why she was even there in the first place. It also allows my thoughts to drift into the idea of how much I adore that fact. I wanted to slip my stressed, drained figure underneath the cool covers and lay beside her. I wanted to run my fingertips down the curve in her scarless back and listen to the giggles she would try hiding from me. I wanted to run my unstable palms through her chocolate-brown hair, lock her hands in mine, and hold that exquisite being in my arms as she fills me with warmth. However, I can't do that right now.

I smile at my drawing thinking about oh-so-beautiful, Ella Buchanan. A sudden, abrupt bang transpires, startling me as I nearly spill the boiling-hot coffee onto my artwork. Missing the piece, the drink reaches my left leg.

"Shit, shit, shit, ow!!" I yell as my body springs off the couch.

Practically sprinting into the living room, Ella's face was giving off a look of dismay. "Fuck, fuck, fuck. Quint, turn on the TV! Quick!" she proclaims.

"My leg is fucking burning!" I scream.

"Quint!!!" El says pointing towards the television.

"Shit, ouch... I will, jesus. Get me some ice or something."

"Turn it on, now." she was no longer scrambling around, frightfully. She was the most intimidating thing I had ever seen.

As Ella runs to the kitchen to get me something for my led, I grab the controller off the coffee table and switch the TV on.

"What channel, El?!" I yell towards the kitchen.

"Four! It's the news, hurry!!" She belts as it echoes slightly.

I click the channel to four.

Breaking news...

Shit.

A man in the Seattle area...

Jimmy. Please be Jimmy.

...was found dead in his apartment...

"Quint, is it on?" Ella asks as she walks out to hand me the ice.

"Yes, shut up." I say nicely as possible.

...after the police looked into the situation, they had found he was poisoned with ricin...

Ella's clenches fist as I say to myself quietly "What's his name? Jesus fucking christ, what is his damn name?"

...unsure of the suspects, *insert name here* must have been poisoned a couple of hours before his death...

Fuck. I throw my hands onto my forehead, resting my elbows on my knees. This can't be right. We killed the wrong man and we didn't even know the guy in the first place. I felt sick to my stomach as I spoke to El "How did this happen?".

"I don't fucking know. It doesn't make sense." she speaks, frustratingly.

"What do we do now, El? I'm so fucking scared." I feel tears on the verge of releasing.

"I wish I knew, Quint. I really wish I knew." she said as she joined me on the couch.

I felt the acid in my stomach begin to bubble as it swam up my throat slowly. Dashing to the bathroom, I throw up all of my troubles into the toilet. I have never felt this hopeless.

Etude

I'm on fire. I am radioactive waste, burning at five thousand degrees, without a chance of being put out. The heat I'm putting off is enough to incinerate anyone within a mile of my blackened flesh. As Quint vomits his insides out in his bathroom, I can't stop hearing that innocent man's name in my ear. I had the perfect shot and, somehow, I missed. It's the assault on Mia all over again. I want to hit something, anything. Punch a hole in the nearest wall, I don't care. I just need to let all of my ferocity out.

Under this blanket of rage lies a sleeping baby of a concept. In the passing minutes, Quentin's black French roast brings my mood to a calming neutral, and the baby awakens and begins to split my head with the sound of its crying. Jimmy knows. I don't know how, but Jimmy knows. Both attempts to hurt him have been countered perfectly. The fact that Minny died as soon as we employed her and that my poison was given to the wrong person when the barista knew intended recipient personally is not a coincidence. Maybe if one had failed, I would believe it, but both? No way in hell. But I still can't quite grasp how.

When Quint finally stumbles out of the bathroom, wiping the puke off of his lips, I can tell from the look in his eyes that he knows what I'm going to tell him.

"He knows, Quint. He fucking knows. He killed Betty, and he poisoned that guy on the TV, Mack...or Mark, or whatever his name is."

He nods, sitting down next to me, his breath awful as I lean in close to him. "It's gotta be someone at the coffee place that's helping him." and then I understand.

During our first meeting with Minny, we were at Ground Zero. Who was the only employee there? Becky. Who was the first person Jimmy talked to three days ago at the coffee shop? Becky. To whom did I give the poisoned mocha to deliver to Jimmy? Becky. Oh. My. God.

I can't contain my fear now. "Quentin, it's Becky. Her and Jimmy are partners. I told him to be prepared, and he is. They've killed twice..." I begin to cry. Again, a rare spectacle, saved for only the most dire circumstances. "...so what's to stop them from killing us?"

They are ahead of us. They know everything. They are powerful, because Jimmy knows everyone, and he has enough money to employ half the Seattle population to protect him. Quentin knows this and, when he looks at me, shocked, I know the words on his rancid lips before they escape. Our only advantage in this situation is that Jimmy isn't aware we're onto him. We have to hit him where he's not expecting, and we have to do it quickly.

"We need to kill him before he kills us."

***

It's been many years since I've set foot in Jimmy's place, but, being my first abode in Seattle, I will never forget the location. I stand on the corner of Terry and Stewart, staring straight up at the Aspira Tower. He lives on the 36th floor. Almost the pretentious ass on top of the skyscraper, on the 37th floor. It seems most of Jimmy can be described with the word almost.

I know he's not home. Streetcar is opening in my hometown of Portland this weekend, so he will oversee the process for the first few days before returning home to leave the cast to their devices for the remainder of their tour. This gives us three days to develop a plan, and we will execute on day four, Jimmy's first full day back home, I assume. The penthouse on the 36th floor our target, and three days to aim, the time to fire is fast approaching.

La Vie en Rose

The thought of Jimmy's breath still occurring on the face of this earth causes my abdomen to turn upside down. The punishment he deserves was completely lent to a harmless Seattle man. A man that didn't get goodbyes or to live the life he should have. I wanted to rewind, edit the inaccuracy of our plan and banish the mistakes from existence. My mind was a bloody sea, overflowing with guilt from this disaster that must be drained before there is no longer flood-able land. I grabbed my leather journal from the table at my bedside, my hands trembling with fear.

<u>Journal Entry 7</u>
February 15th, 2013

I can no longer take the act of failure anymore. My life was a complete failure, along with my dreams, mine and El's plan, my family, my everything. Nothing went as we wanted it to. For all we know, Jimmy is planning to murder us with his twisted stupidity. He obviously knew something was going on and there is no doubt in my mind, all of this was done for nothing. I'm done trying to fix this hell.

I needed to leave. I must leave. As much as I love Ella, I can't stay here and keeping fighting this unwinnable fight. It's doing nothing but making things much worse than they should have been. I don't want to leave this beautiful girl behind. I wanted her to come with me, run away to who knows where. Maybe we could run. We could simply leave Washington to get a place in Portland where her family lives. I'm just ready to move on from this collapsing point and start over.

The real question is, will she move on with me or leave me completely?

I needed to speak to Ella, whether I wanted to or not, to let her know what I think is prime for us. These homicidal acts must stop or else one of us might get mutilated. The unyielding part of this whole situation was trying to persuade El into agreeing with me in the first place. Pulling my phone out of my pocket, I call up Ella.

After 3 buzzes, she picks up "El, we need to talk, *now*".

Lullaby

Day three. With Quentin up in the Aspira Tower, attempting to seduce Jimmy's girlfriend to steal a key to the apartment, I was waiting on the sidewalk underneath it, ready to receive a key from him in an hour or four. Breaking into the apartment would give me an idea of an attack plan. Not even knowing what the condominiums looked like inside, I couldn't very well come to a conclusion. After this day was over, we would only have the night to plan the "Atwell Assault", then we would execute tomorrow at 8 o'clock PM, two hours after Jimmy's flight landed from Portland.

All this extensive detailing going on in my head is really just to distract me from what is going on almost four hundred feet above me. Quint is going to have sex with Mia. Ugh. The very thought is absolutely hideous. It's less about the fact that it's Mia and more about the fact that he's having sex. Over the past months, it's grown very clear that he has feelings for me (who wouldn't?), and that gets to a person after a while. Though I'm still sticking to the story that I find him attractive but am not attracted to him, I still feel rather territorial about the whole situation (not that I'm jealous or anything). Being the closest to him, I feel that if anyone should be the one to play his saxophone, it might as well be me. Not that I want to or anything. Really, I'm not jealous. Really.

Even though I'm not jealous, I need to find something to take my mind off the whole sex situation. The Aspira just happens to be about two blocks away from the Paramount theatre, the other big Broadway theatre in Seattle, somewhat of a rival of the 5th Avenue. Currently showing Wicked, it was my number one choice for a distraction. Being a Saturday and 7:49 PM, the show would be starting soon, so I decided to see if I could get a ticket. Seeing as I was gonna be back with my parents in two or three days, I was burning cash like a drunken sailor. When I arrived at the ticket office, the employee informed me there was a seat in row H open, so I snapped it up. How fitting that my last moment of peace in Seattle was spent in the audience. The spotlight would come soon enough.

Rawhide

Staring up at the Aspira Tower, I prepare myself to go up many flights of stairs. As I'm dragging myself floor by floor, I realize this was all too much. First, Ella completely agrees with me on wanting to leave this hellhole. Second, she turns on the situation and supposes we'll keep going to finish what we had started. Now, I'm expected to sleep with, not only all business Jimmy Atwell's girlfriend, but the girl who thought it would be hilarious to mess with El after her brother's death, just to have a way in Jimmy's home. Did she really deserve to steal something of mine? I'm not ready for this.

Sleeping with someone shouldn't be something one simply does for the pleasure. Putting that much trust into another human's hands should be saved for a girl I'm in love with, not some random woman who is in relations with a damn killer. The thought of sex made me cringe and my hands grow shaky. Everything about sex disgusts me entirely. The sweat dripping from each other's body, the feeling of closeness vanished from one's mind, the meaningless moans, and even worse, not a single touch is added afterward. There is no action of being held tightly by them, no smiles or giggles, with no fingers intertwining together fitting together like the found, missing puzzle piece everyone was searching for.

I want my first time to be something more than that. I find myself desiring the concept of making love. I'm not another object waiting to be pounded on like a female cat in heat. I'm a human being who needs love, warmth, and the touch of one's palms sliding up my back as I kiss her neck softly. Envision the concept of kissing the one you are in love with till the end of time, in your own little world, while brushing your fingers through their crisp hair, holding them as their breath presses against your chest. That's sounds breathtakingly beautiful.

If I didn't have sex with this foolish girl, Mia, I would be a disappointment. I don't think El knows I haven't lost my virginity and I'm terrified to even mention it to her. I'm 34 and I haven't once had sex with another girl and I'm not ready. I'm not ready to give it up to Mia because we need a damn house key to Jimmy's place. Judging by the look on Ella's face, I don't have a choice.

Staring blankly at the door that reads "362: Atwell", I bring my knuckles to the surface, lightly knocking. My heart rate picks up as I hear each faint footstep pulling closer and closer towards the door. The knob turns, cracking the door slightly, a girl's face peeks through.

"Yes?" Mia asks, confused.

"Hey, is Jimmy here? I'm Quentin, his best friend. He hasn't been returning any of my calls or texts and I was wondering if I can get some sheet music I let him borrow." I let out a grin as lies spew from my mouth.

"He's in Portland for a show, but you can come in a look if ya like." she smiles without a care in the world.

Letting myself in, it was odd knowing I have never stepped foot into Jimmy's home. The vibe the condo gave off was entirely sickening. Woods floors covered the place, with windows the size of an entire wall looking down on Seattle, lime-green walls partnered by fake plants located in random areas, and a flat screen television so giant that it might as well be a theatre.

"So... you must be Jimmy's girlfriend?" I question, with a smirk, while pretending to scramble around looking for sheet music.

"Well, I guess, but we're not official. He's gone so often, I don't quite know." she laughs, almost flirtatiously.

"I see."

"Have you found what you're looking for?" Mia asks.

"Not quite." I lie.

"Would you like a drink? I've been so lonely these past couple of days, so it would be nice to talk a little with

someone." she smiles.
"Yes, please." I let out a flirty grin.

My phone buzzes as Mia walks to the kitchen to get drinks. I pull it out to see a text from El. "Seeing a show at the Paramount. Tell me when you're done!"

I text her in reply "Go ahead. Have fun!"

Mia walks back out of the kitchen smiling, holding an orange, citrus-looking drink with lime "Pura vida?"

"What's that?" I ask without any idea what she was giving me.

"Oh, just a recipe from Costa Rica I got off of the internet. Try it!" she hands me the very glamorous drink.

"This is wonderful, thank you." I say after sipping the pura vida.

Sitting herself next to me on the couch, she glances in my eyes as she runs her fingers through my hair. "These drinks sure do taste amazing"

"Um... yes. I love them" I let out an awkward smile.

Her eyes start to move up and down from my lips to my eyes within seconds. Her body pulls closer and closer towards me. "Promise to keep this our little secret" she says rubbing her fingertips gently down my spine, giving me goosebumps.

"I... I promise" I lie to her directly as the nerves in my body twitch uncontrollably and everything seems absolutely amiss.

Mia's eyes close seductively as she moves her left palm up my right arm. Pulling me towards her, she places her lips against mine.
I feel disgusting.

Starting of slowly, the kisses begin to grow more intense. My hands slide up her shirt, pulling it off of her hastily.

This is too much. I've never seen a girl naked in real life before. Holy shit.

She practically rips mine off, immediately springing off the couch and practically prying herself on top of me, kissing me. I find her hands zipping down my pants as my body starts to shiver.

I can't take it. I need Ella.

I pull down her tightly fit, yoga pants as my hands shake uncontrollably. Practically completely naked, her hands reach down my underwear.

I don't love Mia. This needs to stop.

That was the first time I have been touched by another girl. I no longer have any doubt of something I used to be afraid to admit.

I'm in love with Ella Robin Buchanan.

Lullaby ii

I received the text from Quentin during intermission. Having seen the show before when Jimmy was still my companion and would buy me tickets to anything I wanted, I didn't feel obligated to stick around for the grand finale. I'd seen Defying Gravity, so that was all that was necessary.

When I arrived back at the Aspira Tower, Quint was waiting for me at the front door, looking exhausted, his mop of dark hair a mess, topping his sweat covered face. This time, he actually did hug me as soon as he saw me. I could tell he had hated the last couple of hours with a passion, from the tension in his shoulders until they relaxed when I placed my hands on his back. However, he had succeeded in his heroic quest with hours to spare in the day. He handed me the key to Jimmy's apartment as we separated, his eyes looking sunken, as if he hadn't slept in a week.

"His place is disgustingly nice." he tells me. "Hardwood floors, glass walls, expensive liquor everywhere." As he speaks, my heart races for a second before I can think through why. His breath is reeking of alcohol. Absolutely reeking of it. Just like Jimmy's did the night I was...um...alone. I hate it.

Trying to disguise my panic, I take the key from him and signal to follow me inside. As we ascend in the elevator, I can still smell his breath and it makes me sick.

"I'm sorry I made you do that." I tell him quietly.

Floor 5.

"It needed to be done, El."

Floor 9.

"It's just, it made me uncomfortable, so I can't imagine what it was like for you."

Floor 14.

"Ella, it's fine, okay?"
Floor 17
"Are you okay, Quint? You don't seem fine."
Floor 23.
"El, it's just..."
Floor 25
"Yeah, Quint?"
Floor 28.
Silence.
"That was my first time."

Floors 29 through 35 seem like they take an eternity to reach as my face turns scarlet with embarrassment. If I would have known that little bit of information, I never would have asked Quentin to do that. Just...wow. The fact that he had the courage and loyalty to do that for me, for us, is amazing. God, I wish Quint and I had met under different circumstances. If we had met, maybe in high school, there could be a future for us. Maybe we could perform together. The two of us singing while the Buchanan family band plays the blues behind us in front of an empty audience. Maybe we would even start dating, and he would propose to me in a song, and our kids would grow up in a world with jazz, and reruns of Star Trek TOS, and wonderful food, and the perfect family, without knowing the word alone.

Floor 36.

***

I never did respond to that last comment from Quint. I simply stood in silence as the last seven floors passed agonizingly slowly, until the elevator doors opened and I shot out, looking for the correct apartment to enter.

"You're sure she's asleep?" I whisper to him.

He only nods in response, jerking his head towards the entrance marked "362: Atwell". The plaque on the door reminds me of the heading to a made up bible verse, Atwell: 362, where God talks about evil men getting what they deserve.

As we unlock the apartment and step in together, the stink of liquor permeates my head, and I can feel it making me physically ill and exhausted. Quint's description was spot on. Everything that wasn't made of glass was made of stainless steel or hardwood. How could we hit this bastard without him having any warning? Then I'm hit with it.

As I turn to Quint, sparks lit in my eyes (you'll get it in a second), I have the idea.

"Quint, this place is basically a hardwood castle. What does wood do?"

He smiles as he catches on to my imagination.

"Wood burns, Ella."

Part Three:
Finale

Nocturne

Day 4. At the base of the massive 37 story tower, Jimmy's car, a silver and pretentious Audi S8 stands guard at the entrance, frowning up at us as if it knows the plan about to transpire. Jimmy, having arrived back in Seattle two and a half hours earlier on a red-eye, would undoubtedly be asleep. Nearing midnight, dressed in the darkest clothing we owned, Quint and I began to enter the Aspira, less than twenty short minutes away from leaving for Portland and the Buchanan household.

Each with backpacks each containing two small containers of gasoline we had purchased the day before, we didn't look normal by any means, but we didn't look suspicious enough to be stopped. For a change, the two of us are silent. The elevator, during our ascent, is drowned in the noise of our deep breathing, in attempts to steady our nervous hearts, instead of the usually awkwardly spaced conversations, as if we're two teenage actors constantly forgetting our lines. Floors 1-36 fly by within seconds from the anxiety of the impending climax.

Nine and a half years have been building up to these next minutes. It felt like a first date with the love of your life. I know it's odd to be likening that to a murder by arson, but it's a personal comparison and it works for me. God, I'm excited. I'm shaking. I'm hyperventilating. I'm ready to puke. Emotions are mixing together into a seasoned soup of hate, and I was about to take the first delicious bite. I could already taste it running down my throat, filling me with warmth that heats me from the inside out, making my sweat run down my forehead and into my eyes, as revenge and garlic fuse into absolute and wonderful desire.

Mouth watering with anticipation as the elevator doors slide open, revealing the path to the end of our tunnel, where an "X" marks the spot for the gold at the bottom of our black rainbow.

Then we're at the door. "Atwell: 362" staring at us, judging us just like Jimmy's Audi had. I glance at Quint, noticing that he's shaking, and look away before he notices my eyes ever landed on him. As I pull the key from my back pocket, gasoline weighing me down, I can't bring myself to slide it into the lock. Something is going to go wrong.

I.

Can.

Feel.

It.

Chocolate

Turning right after exiting the anxiously long, 36 floors elevator ride, on the left sat the door to Jimmy's. Ella and I come to a stop no less than one foot away from the door that read "362: Atwell". Glancing over at El, whose body was shivering as her fists were clenching, I take a breath. Millions of thoughts ran through my head as if they were dancing children on a playground playing a game of tag. Today was the day Jimmy Atwell, who was once my best friend, goes to hell. I found it very resistant to comprehend what was meant to happen tonight. In the dark condo before me, Mr. Atwell would soon burn in flames as his body cooks to a crisp black. My mind began to ache as further thoughts spewed from my right ear to the left. James Leonardo Atwell will no longer ruin others lives. Instead, he'll suffer as the gasoline lights before us. I'm not the Quentin Harris I was a year ago and I have officially revealed who I truly am. I don't know if I'm willing to accept these notions and activities yet.

Still staring blankly at the door, terrified of what is to happen before me, my hands grow shakier. All I wanted to do was interweave my fingers with the girl I'm in love with. If tonight was my last night alive, I needed to have that satisfaction. Being held by Ella would fill the emptiness placed within my chest looking at the door to hell. I find myself creeping my fingers closer to hers, trembling. Closing my eyes, I grab her hand, pulling her near my waist.

"Quint..." she looks startled, pulling her hand away from the puzzle.

"El, fucking quit it. I'm terrified right now and I need to feel close to someone and the only someone I have is you. Hold my hand. We aren't in elementary school, I don't have cooties" I grab her hand for a second time, sternly. "Unlock the door, El."

Pulling the key out of her left pocket, she pushes the key into the lock, turning it to the right until a slight click is released.

"Are you ready, Quint?" she says with a mischievous look in her eyes.

"I'm ready, El." I look directly in her eyes without a trace of a smile as she opens the door slowly.

Walking into Jimmy's place, the darkness is pleasuring. It wasn't pure blackness due to the wall-sized windows overlooking the city lights. Looking down at the beautiful, restless Seattle, Washington the towering buildings consist of random windows full of brightness versus ones of complete darkness. The place was exactly the same as it had been from that night. Hardwood floors taking up space from corner to corner, a giant flat screen, various alcoholic beverages placed on tables, and the disgustingly fake plants.

Ella and I sit down on the green couch in the middle of the over-sized living room. Pulling the backpacks off of our shoulders, I begin laying out our plan entirely in my head. I tiptoe to the master bedroom where I would suspect Jimmy was sleeping as Ella gets items situated. Cracking the door open just a sliver, I peek one eye through to make sure he is asleep. The door making a slight creak, Jimmy's body turns from left to right, but he still seemed to be in deep sleep.

"He's asleep, El." I tell Ella as I walk back out to the living room, slowly.

"Good. Grab some gasoline from your bag and pour a bit by the stove." she says pointing towards my backpack.

"Alright, El." I pull it out of my bag and tiptoe to the kitchen.

I hear a toilet flush and my heart begins to race, palms sweating, and I rush to El before I got the chance to pour a single drop.

"I thought you said he was asleep, you idiot!" she yells through a whisper.

"I swear to god, he fucking was." I feel panic run through my body.

As footsteps come closer, El runs behind a table hiding herself before I get the chance to move even a centimeter. A shadow is presented before me in the corner of the living room, all business.

Fuck.

Nocturne ii

As I dive behind the table, I hear Jimmy's somewhat inebriated voice drawing at Quentin.

"What the hell...?" As I cringe at the sound of that voice, the voice I heard that night he raped me, I hear him rushing into the kitchen, presumably to find a weapon. Swearing, Quint dives into the kitchen as well. The one advantage we have at this point is that I don't think Jimmy is completely aware of my presence in his home. I hear a scramble on the kitchen floor, Jimmy's bare feet smacking with hard packing sounds on the hardwood, as the saxophone player's Oxford's squeak in an unpleasant shout.

I leap up from the table, turning it over, glasses and bowls from a rushed dinner falling and crashing to the floor, the glass shattering over the floor. As I enter the kitchen, heart in my throat, Quint and Jimmy are caught in a lock, the latter's armed wrapped around the throat of the former. Quint sputtering for breath, I rush to his aid, pounding my elbow into Jimmy's nose with all of my strength. As the blood pours from his nose, spilling onto the wood floor, he releases Quentin. As Quint recedes into the living room from where he dropped it seconds earlier, Jimmy, climbing up from his knees in front of me, grabs a knife from the block on his counter.

"QUINT!" I scream as he strikes out at me, the bite of a wild animal as it catches its prey for a long awaited supper. I am the gazelle, jumping back from the cheetah as it pounces, its wicked teeth snapping at me, spit flying from its gullet.

As I back into the fridge, I duck underneath another swing that collides with the metal, sending the knife spinning from his hand. The knife, flying towards my face like a javelin, cuts me under my left eye and my face grows warm with blood. Now that the knife has spiraled away from us, I sprint out of the kitchen towards the saxophone player as he pours gasoline hurriedly over the floor, checking to make sure the coast is clear and no wild animals are hunting him.

I search the room as fast as I can for a weapon before I'm brought down by Jimmy's tackle. As I'm pinned down by 180 pounds of animal, rips Jimmy off of my body, throwing him across the floor with so much effort I can feel the tension in his back and arm muscles. Running around the dog pile of the two men, writhing on the floor, I run back into the kitchen, almost slipping on blood. As I slide into the fridge, my face smacks against it, my blood smearing the cold metal as I look for another weapon. Before I can grab another knife from the block, I spot a cast iron skillet, encrusted with that evening's dinner, waiting for me on the stove top. Grabbing the skillet and running with all my energy back into the living room, I take note that I'll need to clean my blood off of the fridge before we depart.

"QUINT, MOVE!!!" I screech, holding the skillet above my head threateningly. He takes a few more seconds to detach himself from the steaming wild animal before leaping up and crawling as far away and as quickly as possible, his leg bleeding, I'm guessing from another one of Jimmy's weapons. As I bring the pan down onto Jimmy's head, as if he's a pig ready to be cut up and made into bacon, just to be fried by my mother on the morning of my graduation in a cast iron skillet just like this one, I feel a crack through my hands as his head crunches underneath my swing, sending him into a deep state of unconsciousness.

As Quint stares up at me, shocked by what I just did, and with a "deer in the headlights" look plastered on his face, I gesture to the can of gasoline, signaling that we need to get to work. Time's a wastin', boy.

Chocolate ii

My lower right thigh still bleeding and aching terribly, I find myself limping to Ella and Jimmy's seemingly lifeless body in the kitchen. Looking at El, I realize that her left cheek, right below her eye, had been slashed by something.

"El, are you okay?" I ask in a panic.

"I'm fine! Are you okay?" she asks worryingly.

"I'll be okay, I think." my mouth utters.

Pulling Ella up off of the ground, we walk over to the couch. So much just happened and it was extremely spine-tingling. There was still actions ahead of us and it hurt to even think about it. One goes through so much pain just to get revenge on someone so corrupt, so pernicious. Ella pulls her knees into her chest as her shoulders convulse.

"Quint, this is so hard." I can hear El's voice pushing the tears down her throat.

"I know, El. We need to finish what we've already started." I place my hands on her knees as she looks at me. Although we were practically in complete darkness, her eyes spoke to me. Her engaging brown eyes lit up this entire room before a single flame was lit before us.

"We need to move Jimmy's body to his bed as if he's been sleeping." I tell Ella as she cools herself down.

"Let's do this." she says as her eyes illuminate the room even more.

We walk over to the kitchen to Jimmy's all business, unconscious body.

"Grab his feet, El."

As I lift him up by his shoulders, we meander around various pieces of furniture, skidding across the hardwood floor below us. Entering his bedroom, we set him on the ground beside his unmade, king-sized bed. I pull the crimson covers towards the right and fluff the pillow (how nice of me, right?).

"Go get a wet rag from his bathroom." I tell Ella as she stares at me and nods.

As Ella hands me the wet rag, I wipe the the blood from Jimmy's slightly cracked skull. He looked so peaceful and it sickened me. El and I lift him up by his ankles and wrists, setting him on the bed. I cover him up, leaving his left leg out to lose suspicion.

"Quint, time for gasoline." an evil grin appears on Ella's face.

"I'm on it."

Walking into the living room, still holding the bloody rag, I spot our backpacks sitting beside the couch, untouched, and the gasoline I was about to use earlier was on the table above the bags. Unzipping the small pouch in the front, I pull out the matches and place them in my back pocket, replacing them with the bloody rag. Grabbing the gasoline off the table, I walk back into the bedroom where I find Ella standing beside Jimmy. I have never seen her look that scarred, that disgusted.

"Give it to me." Ella insists as she sticks her right hand out towards me.

I hand the red container to El, her hands trembling. I watch her as she surrounds Jimmy's bedside with gasoline. I observe as liquid splashes against the ground and the light in Ella's eyes grows even brighter. She walks out of his bedroom, pouring random dashes of gas throughout his condo. Placing the emptied container back in her backpack I look at her.

"El..."

"Quint, it's time." she says moving closer towards me.

I pull the matches out of my back pocket, shivering. I pull on Ella's shoulder, leading her towards the door. I stare at Jimmy's apartment feel rage build up inside me. It was time for that bastard to burn to death. I strike the match three times before receiving a fire of any sort.

"Close your eyes, El." I wanted to kiss her. I have waited months for this very moment. I have wanted to show Jimmy what he deserves and it's my turn to get what I'm worthy of.

"Count backwards from three" I tell her, match in my left hand as I place my right palms against her waist.

"Three...Two..." I place my quivering lips against hers, cutting off her words in that very instant, throwing the match across the room.

As I release my lips Ella looks directly in my eyes and I see the room's burning reflection in her bronze irises.

"One."

Nocturne iii

While Quint goes to retrieve the gasoline from our backpacks, I, in turn take my own detour. Wetting down a cloth from the kitchen, I saturate the bloodied streak on the fridge with water and scrub as best I can to remove any trace of my DNA from the surface. It's obvious the police will figure out this fire was by no means an accident. However, it doesn't hurt to deceive them for at least a few hours while we settle in to Portland life. They will see his skull has been cracked, and they will see that the fire was started with gasoline, but we will be long gone before the dead-end of a manhunt begins.

Sixty seconds later, as I'm pouring gasoline all over the godforsaken house, I think of Mia's reaction when she returns to the burnt crisp of a home. The baby bird returns to its nest, just to find its mother has been killed by the poacher, the nest as empty as the day it was created. No more protection, no more security. I almost feel sorry for this girl. She'll have to live alone now, after living off of Jimmy's money and semen, I'm sure, for quite a long time.

As I return to the living room, Quint is waiting for me, his hand in his back pocket, ready to retrieve the box of matches.

"El..."

"Quint, it's time."

This fire. This fire had been building inside me for so long, and I was about to breath it out upon Jimmy's life, engulfing the castles, knights, and damsels in distress, every man, woman, and child running for their lives.

Out of nowhere, Quentin's voice whispers in my ear. "Close your eyes, El." Puzzled, I do as he says, just for a millisecond forgetting why we're here, to breathe fire and to send the townspeople running.

"Count backwards from three." As I grin and begin to do as he says, getting only to two, I feel his lips against mine. Oh my god. My heart is bursting out my mouth as he kisses me, softly, without passion, just with sweetness. Before it even begins, it's over, as we pull away from each other, and in Quentin's blue eyes I see fire. The desire leaps back in forth across his face as the living room begins to go up in flames, as if a mist over the sea is burning, the sky growing red with wine dark plumes of heat. I remember this being the only time I felt truly attracted to Quint. The only time I didn't regret the kiss we had just shared, amongst the sparks flying around us.

As we leave the condo hurriedly, leaving everything behind us, the only detail I remember was Quint bumping into the door frame as we stepped out, smearing the blood from his thigh over the polished metal, oblivious to what he had done. Well, I remember two details. The second was not stopping to clean the blood off of the door frame.

Stuck in the Middle

Flames explode from Jimmy's condo as Ella and I sprint towards the elevator in complete panic. The fire alarm ringing at a pitch so shrill, I cringe as every screech belts out. I find myself banging on the arrow pointing down several times before realizing the elevator shuts down when there's a fire.

"Fuck, El. We have to go down the stairs." I feel the tension in my knuckles grow faintly stronger.

"Shit, shit, shit!" Ella utters as she scrambles around looking for the staircase.

Doors slam as people begin to flood the halls around us on the 36th floor, swimming through the parade of fish, scurrying aimlessly. A man, who must have been at least 300 hundred pounds, sweat dripping from his red t-shirt, makes his way through to the staircase around the corner from the elevator (I can't believe we didn't see that).

My immediate impulse to grab ahold of Ella's hand, so I don't lose her. Losing her would cause the world to crumble into millions of pieces. The lands within the waters of Earth would cave in as whirlpools of the deep blue sea tumble over the one another. All the life on, what were once continents, would be swallowed by the blistering heat within this wicked planet. I can't tell you what would happen after that. No one knows what it's like to have no life, but the ones without it. Whether it be unabridged blackness without any way of escaping from a cavernous sleep or pure luminosity as a second life lies before us, we just don't know. Although I'm am insanely curious, I'm entirely transfixed about the whole situation.

My hand slips through Ella's as people flood down the 36 flights of stairs.

Floor 34

I feel Ella's palm beat with sweat as the people

surround her, ear to ear.

Floor 31

Pulling El towards me, I signal to her that I want to slow down. I was tired of hearing humans breathing in a rhythm so unsatisfying everywhere we move.

Floor 25

As the people clear from my vision, my brain spins around frivolously.

"El..."

Floor 19

My legs began to grow sore, my heart pumping like no other, and the muttering of people started to increase in volume the further we went down the steps.

"I'm scared, El." Still holding her hand, I squeeze it when those words fly from my mouth.

"It's okay, Quint. I've got you" she let out a cheesy smile to hide the anxiety.

Floor 1

The lobby was completely packed as the fish were still trying to spring from the sea. Ella and I placed ourselves at the back hoping to receive little attention (thank god Ella was a fantastic actress). She could pretend to be normal so well. She smiled at those who would ask if we were okay. A tear even flew down her cheek when others were talking about all their stuff being completely ruined, but I know she doesn't care one bit.

Finally making our way through the crowd, we exit the Aspira Tower. Burn Mr. Atwell. Fucking Burn.

Scherzo

Apartment 362 in flames above us, windows popping and shards of safety glass shattering to the ground around our feet, we were running so hard, our throats were burning, acid melting our insides as the symphony's chorus played in my ears, deafening me against the Seattle skyline. I can hear the whine of fire engines many blocks away as they speed toward us in the night, their red flash lighting up the sky, that was as black as my heart. Quint, next to me, was trying to speak as words caught in his throat, choking him against his will.

I couldn't focus on the chaos, however. My mind was lost on the 36th floor of the tower, wanting so bad to forget about the spot of blood, so thickly ripe with DNA that would give Quentin away so quickly we might not even get to Portland. Deep in the fibre of my being, I know my instinct was correct. To fully have freedom when I get home, to fully forget about this huge piece of my life, Quint couldn't be with me, he couldn't ride in the right seat as I drove us home. I needed to leave this godforsaken city I had come to look upon as purgatory and, in turn, the saxophone player behind with it.

So I suppose I'm glad Quentin's blood splattered against the door, encrusted maroon upon the wall, ready to be discovered. His impending imprisonment will set me free, even if I never see him again. I do regret the necessity for revealing Quint's involvement, but it must be done. If there are no immediate suspects, police will start turning to Jimmy's friends, which will eventually lead them to me. Just as a game show must have a winner, the police must find someone guilty. I'm simply not strong enough to let that someone be me.

I know I've said this before, but if I had three wishes, they would be spent on moving Quint and I's first meeting somewhere else, sometime else, and somehow else. Quentin George Harris and Ella Robin Buchanan are the perfectly dynamic duo, brought together, two celestial brothers touching but just once, in an absolutely and completely imperfect universe. The clarinet and the saxophone, finally parting, after a duet several months long, onto opposite wings of the stage, with no audience to see us go or standing ovation to wish us farewell, and all at once, I feel rage that it has to end this way. The unstoppable fury drives me even farther, ahead of Quint as I sprint with all my might away from the burning castle, a dragon broken free of its bindings and setting off into the darkness without even a glance behind.

Stuck in the Middle ii

Nearly five days ago, the man who was once my best friend, Jimmy Atwell, the trombone player, and the director of such fabulous shows, received payment for his ghastly acts of abomination. His body burned atrociously, blackening like one had left grilled cheese on the stove, walked out of the kitchen, and carelessly forgot about it even existing in the first place. Later, one finds the scorched sandwich without a single trace of life presented before them. The toast is completely tenebrous, refusing to let the slightest speck of appetizing characteristics shine.

El and I agreed to wait a few days before contacting each other after the incident and it didn't irritate me as much as I thought it would. I got to hold the girl I'm in love with through something so full of hatred and revenge. Our lips pulled in together like magnets before something so incredibly horrid took place. I was able to feel closer to an artwork so beautiful, nothing in existence can compare. It was going to be okay.

The was no longer trembling within my hands or sweat crawling from my palms. I am no longer scared of what is ahead of me. It's time to create a painting. I'm ready to express all these jumbled feelings onto a canvas, splattering paint inch by inch.

I pull out my easel and an unused canvas from underneath my empty, creased bed. Searching anxiously through various drawers consisting of old cassettes, CD's, movies I haven't watched in ages, and mail from who knows how long ago, I finally come across my paint brushes. These brushes, the Rosemary and Co utensils before me, were absolutely flawless. Not worrying about perfection in the piece I was about to create, I select a random brush. Dipping it into the orange, I splatter drops rapidly across the canvas feeling the heat within my soul build up. Soon, red was slashed against the masterpiece, yellow, black even.

Aspira. I call this burning artwork, *Aspira.*

Scherzo ii

Four days after the fire, as police are running rampant over two blocks, looking for the culprit, the arson having destroyed all the condos on the 36th floor, as well as the penthouses on the 37th, Jimmy being the only casualty. Well, other than the many millions of dollars of property damage, that is. Still not able to erase the vision of Quint's blood on Jimmy's wall, I knew the investigators would catch on soon to the fact that it belonged to someone other than the owner of the house. Thus, I had convinced him to stay living at his apartment for a few days while I waited for the police to seek him out.

Over the past nights, I have had nightmares, so utterly terrifying I wake up sweating. Jimmy's burning corpse, stumbling its way to my bedroom and burning a hole in the wall, only to crawl into bed with me. As the body's flame quickly consumes my bed, taking me with it, my blood boiling as I bake like a lobster in the middle of a stove top, Quint's voice echoes in my ears. I don't remember the words he screams at me, but I can tell they're words of hate, cries of fear as I leave him behind for somewhere better.

When I awaken from the nightmares, the covers, down to the sheets, have disappeared onto the floor, and I lay in a puddle of moist mattress, my hyperventilation only making me colder. I sometimes wonder that I might be waking because of the lack of temperature, not the nightmare itself.

What would keep me up at night would be being in Quentin's place. Relieved that he has no idea he's a blind man standing on a railroad track, ready to be split in half, I can't imagine what it would be like to know his fate. Knowing that the police will discover evidence that points them towards you, knowing that you will be caught, knowing that will be charged with arson as well as first degree murder, and you will be sent to death row, would kill me, stress, guilt, anxiety, fear, and rage being blended into the fiercest smoothie ever tasted by man. I'm glad I'm not in his shoes. I'm glad he doesn't know the shoes he's in. I'm glad I'll be gone before he realizes it. People say a parent should never outlive their child. Well, a clarinetist should never outlive a saxophonist. An Ella should never outlive her Quentin.

Black as Night

The mist in the streets of busy Seattle, Washington surrounded me while the cement was blanketed with puddles of rain from last night's storm. Strolling along the sidewalk, vehicles splashed water against other vehicles like children having a water balloon fight, striking each other uncontrollably. The pedestrians filling the walkway were bundled up, wearing fur and pea coats while scarves squeezed their necks tightly for warmth. Almost everyone is holding umbrellas above themselves to block all the rain from hitting their shoulders.

My body covered by only a duffel (I don't need an umbrella. I'm a man), my knuckles grab tight onto the piece I had painted the other night that I had bagged so it wouldn't get wet. I called up the manager of Ground Zero and they agreed that they would have my artwork put up in the shop if they think it's worthy. This depiction was one of the most unblemished images I have ever created. The flames presented in the picture were absolutely breath taking. There was no way in hell they wouldn't put it up in their shop. In my other hand, I grab a hold of "Red". I haven't placed a single finger on my saxophone since the day I was searching for Ella. The last piece I had played was Feelin' Good and now that everything is finally over, it's time to perform again.

I turn at the corner of 6th and Virginia to Ground Zero as a rush of satisfaction hits me. When I walk in there, Jimmy won't be sitting there, holding his trombone, all business. Even better, I don't have to sit around, counting light bulbs, waiting for the bastard to get here. James Atwell no longer has the ability to ruin my life minute by minute. I could feel a grin appearing across my face just thinking about it. I don't have to listen to his excuses in that annoying tone of voice or order his drinks for him because he doesn't have the energy to do it himself, even though he had his own two legs.

I walk into a coffee shop that was almost completely empty, setting my things down by the stage. My shoulders, now, release from any sort of tension in my body. The feeling I get every time I enter Ground Zero, warms my chest up like a marshmallow being roasted over a campfire. An unfamiliar barista was working at "The Bar". It was really nice to see a new face.

"Hey there" I let out a grin as I walk near the cash register.

"Hi, what would you like?" A sweet tone is let out of her mouth as she places her hand on the register.

"Just my regular. Sixteen ounce coconut white mocha, but make it 3 shots." My lips curl.

"Gotcha. That would be $3.16" she struggles opening the machine.

I hand her the cash and walk over to the other end to receive my drink. After, a wait that is much longer than usual, she yells out the name of the drink as if there were other people here (she is too funny). Thanking her, I take a sip of the mocha, disappointed by the lack of flavor.

I walk over to the stage to grab my painting. "Hey! Uh..." I shout to the barista trying to figure out .

"Layla. My name is Layla."

"Oh... Layla! I'm not sure if the manager told you, but I'm supposed to give my painting to you to have it looked at to be put up." I tell her.

"Alright." she grabs the painting from my hands, placing it behind "The Bar".

I unpack my sax as people start to flow in every couple of minutes. It felt so invigorating to hold "Red" again. I step onto the stage as confidence rushes through my system. Pressing down the keys and setting my lips onto the mouthpiece, the instrument lets out a roar. The people throughout the shop come to a complete stop as the room grows dark. There's was no longer another being sitting next to me, ruining my spotlight. Although I had practically felt alone before, it is finally true. It was my time to shine and nothing was going to stop me.

Then, a light forms in the corner of my right eye, near the door of Ground Zero. It was Ella. I felt my heart rate picking up as I caught a glimpse of her beauty. It felt like life had rewinded to the day that was supposed to be our first date. This is how it should have been. No Jimmy in sight, with "Red" playing beautifully as El smiles hearing her favorite tune. I could see her lips beginning to move as if she wanted to sing, but she was holding back. I want her to let that sensational voice of her shine as I played along, fabulously. God, that girl was the best thing I had ever seen. She was prettier than any of my art, prettier than my music, prettier than fire, prettier than everything.

I move on to the next piece titled Your Heart Is As Black as Night, while El finds a seat. It finally felt like everything was laying out the way it should have been. After this performance, I could go sit with her and chat about jazz, she can educate me about musicals, and then we could go on a walk. I'll grab her hand as she laughs at my cheesy jokes. She'll pull away until I insist she held my hand. How perfect.

I feel my lips curling into a smile as the reed still sits in my mouth, but suddenly there is no light. Darkness fills the room like the earth on a splendid day when a cloud flits across the sun. It truly was as black as night.

It's gonna be okay, Quint. Smile.

Prelude

The Buchanan family is not religious, but we do have religions. Today is a day that satisfied all three of them. The day of Emerald City Comic-con, nerds from all over the Pacific Northwest gathered in various costumes of varying degree of intensity, including those of the Star Trek persuasion, mixing with the regular Washingtonian folk, going about their everyday chores, all business. Before leaving Seattle, I had made reservations at a wonderful restaurant named Bar del Corso for a sit down meal with octopus and pizza, by far the best Italian food that's ever passed my lying lips. And, of course, here I am currently, in Ground Zero, listening to the best saxophone playing I've heard in a long time.

A new barista fusses over the espresso machine as she makes my Cuban mocha, apologizing for the delay, undoubtedly caused by her lack of experience (Becky, the employee I theorized was informing Jimmy of our plans, promptly quit after said director suddenly became deceased. Hmm...I wonder why?). When the drink is finally finished, after three minutes of struggle, I lay back in a roomy armchair, listening to the tenor sax sing Cry Me a River, without a care in the world. As I finish the poorly made coffee, locked in eye contact with Quint (smiling, of course), I can't help but glance out the door. Making sure red and blue lights aren't about to blind everyone in the room, you know?

As the melancholy melody comes to a close, the audience of five, including me, applaud lightly. As the clapping ends, I run quickly up to the stage, ready to hug Quint one last time. I'm prepared to wrap my arms around his neck, less than a yard away, when I hesitate, grinding to a halt. Quint, knowing my intention, had begun to crack smile, his crooked teeth shining at me like morning's first flight. Now the smile dropped away, just as my speed toward him did. Without a word, I reach into my pocket, dropping a quarter into the saxophone case before winking and turning away, my heart sinking, disguised by my untrustworthy smirk. I hear him chuckling quietly as his lips move back to his mouthpiece, starting to play a song I've never heard before. A minor piece, that seems to almost harmonize with itself. It's haunting, black. Something you might hear in a crime movie, or during a dark romance scene.

Just as I'm falling in love with the song, red and blue lights flash my eyes before I can return to my seat. As soon as the police enter Ground Zero, I'm out the door, getting bumped by an officer or two on the way out.

What I am doing is worse than death. It would have been more human to shoot Quint in the head, as he looks off into a lake, his final reflection smiling back at me. Death is always tragic, but this was more. This was a man that had saved my life, in all styles of heroicness, more times than anyone ever had. If death was a glass falling onto the floor, shattering into a million shards, then this minute, these awful sixty seconds, must be an entire museum of glass works falling into a canyon.

As the symphony came to a close, I didn't hear the songbird hidden inside the saxophone, I didn't hear the police sirens, I didn't hear my own footsteps on the pavement as I ran from death. All I heard was the orchestra, the most beautiful chords, the most simple melodies a cacophony in my brain, splitting me at the seams until the last note sounded. Tubas supporting the band, strings playing at the edges, adding fringe as the woodwinds flurried around the brass, trumpets blasting like cannons two octaves above the score. The standing ovation is only silence as the lights on the stage fade to black, the color of my heart echoing around the city, without a hope of light.

I don't know how, but someday, I will die. I may be shot, I may be killed by a long disease, a car might run over me, and I may commit suicide. In any end, I hope there is an afterlife.

I hope Quentin George Harris is there.

I hope he forgives me for what I did.

I hope he believes me when I say I'm sorry.

That pleasure which is at once the most pure, the most elevating and the most intense, is derived, I maintain, from the contemplation of the beautiful. Thus, the feeling at the end of the symphony, my heart matching pitch with the nighttime, must be derived from the destruction of the beautiful, coffee in my hand, running like a coward towards the light, without the courage to join my love against the dark.

My love?

I never thought I'd say that. What's gotten into me?

Yes, my love. That's the one thing I don't regret.

SECTION 1: CULTURES

1.Spartans

2.The Rarámuri

3.Roman Gladiators

4.Wrestlers of Ancient India

5.Ancient China

6.Irish Collar & Elbow Wrestling

7.Wixarika Peyote Pilgrimage

8.The Bajau

SECTION 2: PEOPLE

SECTION 3: MISCELLANEA

CULTURES

1. The Spartans

“They were the only men in the world with whom war brought a respite in the training for war." ~Plutarch

In September of 480 BC, a small force of 300 Spartans and a handful of auxiliaries held the mountain pass of Thermopylae against 300,000 Persian invaders. Standing shoulder to shoulder to the last man, each stood defiant in the face of certain death and sacrificed his life in defense of his people and his homeland without hesitation. On that day the world learned what Sparta was about, and many have been chasing that elusive sense of purpose and dedication ever since.

A society famed for its austerity, discipline, fitness and equality, Sparta has captured the imagination of the world for thousands of years. Despite their prominent place in the public imagination, much is unknown about the Spartans today. A secretive, isolated and enigmatic people, they were highly mysterious and frequently romanticized even in their own time. They lived separate from the other Greeks, spoke their own language and closed off their culture to outsiders. They forced their children to endure cold, hunger and brutal physical training, however they also discovered democracy before Athens, valued philosophy more than their neighbors and the women of Sparta were more free than anywhere in the world, largely running things while the men trained and fought.

Spartan training began at birth when infants were inspected by the state, with those deemed unfit being left to the elements and animals on Mount Taygetus. At age 7, boys were surrendered by their mothers to the agoge training program where they were trained in combat, athletics, history, survivalism and philosophy. Of those who survived and completed the agoge, the most promising were selected to serve in the krypteia; rangers who patrolled the mountain frontiers barefoot with only a dagger, expected to be completely self-sufficient in their survival and procurement of food. At age 30, his training would be complete.

The citizens of Sparta, both male and female, placed great value on physical fitness, training and culture. While the Athenians were writing comedies or debating politics, the Spartans were training for war. A Spartan's sole purpose in life was to train to be a better Spartan, preparing for the eventual day when he would give his life without hesitation for his homeland. Daily exercise was a part of life: during their suicidal three day battle against the Persians at the Hot Gates, some say that Leonidas and the 300 woke up early every morning and did their calisthenics routines before the days fighting began (even on the last day of battle when they were fully encircled, all were wounded and most were without weapons or shields). And on the final day, after three days of fighting outnumbered 1,000 to 1, as tens of thousands of arrows poured down on the shieldless, weaponless Spartans, the last clutch of survivors would still have the strength, endurance and sheer force of will to charge directly into the source of the arrow fire, penetrating into the line of elite Persian Immortals and killing several of the enemy with their bare hands and teeth before being overwhelmed. The heroism and physical capability demonstrated that day surpassed even the retelling of the final stand depicted in the movie '300', a true example of truth exceeding fiction.

The Spartans believed physical training was the key to attaining such levels of mental and physical fortitude, and they refused to neglect it. Based on archeological evidence, their participation in various ancient games, classical authors, secondary references, reports of their military practices and historical extrapolations, Spartan training consisted of the following dynamics:

•Pankration: ancient mixed martial arts, used both in sport and in war. The victor at the Olympic Games was often a Spartan, as was the case at the other ancient games of the Hellenes.

•Ancient Kettlebell and Dumbbell Training: known from Spartan archeological finds, the haltere was an ancient stone weight used as a kettlebell and dumbbell.

•Running: Spartans could run. Long, fast or both. They trained long distance running as well as sprints, with and without their armor and shield. The victor of the armored foot race held in the ancient Olympics was most often a Spartan.

•Strongman: according to records of games and ancient authors, the lifting and carrying of stones and logs in a manner similar to modern strongman movements was utilized to build strength and endurance. They also enjoyed participating in team strength competitions, such as tugowar, shield wall pushes or even a game where two competing teams seek to push each other off a small island.

•Throwing: stones, javelins and discus were thrown to build explosive power as well as in completion.

•Rucking: Spartan military training consisted of forced marches in 60 lbs. of bronze armor with a pack filled with multiple days of food and supplies.

•Gymnastics and Calisthenics: visiting observers noted that gymnastics and bodyweight exercises were staples of Spartan training, in both men and women. They allegedly completed them every morning without fail, even pregnant women.

•Phalanx training: moving, maneuvering and pushing against resistance with shields while maintaining formation as a phalanx, in full weapons and armor. A phalanx could even be tasked by training officers to push against a tree until it was uprooted, a common training practice in the era of phalangites.

Spartan 'programming', or 'workout routines', is as mysterious as the rest of their ways, a secret even in their own time. Many have tried to sell fitness programs using Spartan imagery or marketing, but the truth is we don't have much concrete evidence of their specific training practices. However based on archeology, the limited contemporary accounts and their participation in certain sporting events (Spartans won many strength, speed and athletic events, so it was safe to assume they trained said events in the secret halls and fields of Sparta), their physical training routine would've likely been composed of a daily morning calisthenics routine combined with organized strength and conditioning and military training, hunting or athletics later in the day. We do know that they trained everyday without fail, possibly using the fourday 'tetrarch' structure utilized across Ancient Greece:

A feasible reconstruction, consistent with the known facts, would look something like:

•Day 1: high intensity workout with logs, stones and sandbags.
•Day 2: long run in full bronze armor, followed by pankration training.
•Day 3: gymnastics and calisthenics workout for movement, coordination and proprioception.
•Day 4: haltere training, resembling standard kettlebell and dumbbell work.
•Additional conditioning: hunting, phalanx drills, swimming, athletics, martial dance and tug o'war.

Diet:
The Spartan diet was as austere as the rest of their culture. There was a great ceremony around the dining experience, as Spartan men lived in communal barracks and dined together in a mess hall known as the syssitia. However when it came to the diet itself, moderation and nutritional density were the ruling principles. To give an example, in the ancient world wheat was the preferred crop of the wealthy due to its rich taste while barley, earthier in taste, was the food of the poor. Spartans, aware of its greater nutritional value and eschewing taste, preferred barley as their

primary carbohydrate source. Another example can be seen in the Spartans' preference for wild game meat while the rest of Ancient Greece dined on fattier cuts from domesticated livestock like lamb and beef, or in their insistence upon eating just two meals a day instead of the four daily meals that was customary throughout the rest of Greece. NonSpartan visitors to Spartan dining halls gave accounts of being hard pressed to finish their unflavored and unseasoned meals, with a particular dread being held for the infamous Spartan 'black soup' made of boiled blood and vinegar.

The most common sources of protein on Spartan plates would've been venison, boar, goat, beef, fish, hare, wildfowl and pigeon. Common fats were fat sources were cheese, olives, lamb, yogurt, nuts. As mentioned, barley was the primary carbohydrate source along with dry figs, honey, legumes and peas. The Spartans even utilized supplementation in the form of their black soup (pig's blood, vinegar and salt), Ironwort mountain tea (for recovery and wound cleaning) and regular use of fasting to promote physical and mental resilience.

"To develop a tolerance for pain, the Spartan youth were deprived of certain luxuries. For instance, during the agoge, Spartan boys were never given shoes. In time, their feet would grow hardy and strong. It is reported by Xenophon that a barefooted Spartan soldier could outrun and out climb any other Greek citizen clad with shoes. Additionally, the boys were given only one garment of clothing. They were regularly subjected to extreme cold, all while only wearing a single cloak. In this way the young soldiers would gain a tolerance to the elements.
They were given minimal food, not so little that they would ever suffer from the sharp pangs of hunger, but never enough that their body would be completely satisfied. This was, again, a way to condition the boys for the pains of hunger and allow them to fight all the more ferociously on an empty stomach."

2. The Rarámuri

Living in widely scattered settlements in Northern Mexico, the Rarámuri are considered the best endurance runners on the planet. They frequently run up to 200 miles at a time over mountains and canyons at high elevation for the sake of communicating with other villages, hunting or transportation. When running they wear only their traditional sandals, known as huaraches which has inspired a good deal of scientific study, academic debate and birthed an entire market of "barefoot shoes".

However distance running isn't just a daily chore for the Raramuri: it's also a spiritual pursuit, a sport and a method for hunting and waging war. Common sporting events include rarajipari, a relay race where balls are kicked, which can last anywhere from a few hours to a couple of days without break. And while they commonly hunt with the bow and arrow, the Rarámuri also practice persistence hunting: the practice of pursuing prey over prolonged time and distance until it collapses from exhaustion, usually deer and turkey.

Their diet is built around traditional staples of corn, bean, and squash, with deer, turkey, squirrel and fish as primary protein sources. They make an 'energy drink' from chia seeds, and corn beer flavored with herbs, known as 'Tesgüino', is a cultural staple at rain fiestas, harvest ceremonies and races. The tribe also grows tobacco and uses the psychedelic peyote cactus as a spiritual guide, said in legend to have been shown to the people by a blue deer.

The Rarámuri were one of the few tribes never conquered by the Spanish nor were they ever converted to Catholicism, mounting fierce resistance from their home high in the inaccessible mountains. Centuries later, revolutionary Pancho Villa would use Rarámuri scouts for their ability to cover vast distances of rough terrain on foot. However modern threats to the tribe include being forced to act as drug runners for cartels, who take advantage of their long distance running abilities, as well as water contamination from mining (something noted as early as 1556) and deforestation from illegal logging.

3. Roman Gladiators

Aelius Galenus, better known as Galen (129216 AD), was a Greek physician and researcher in the Roman Empire. A personal physician to emperors, he is one of the most accomplished medical researchers in history. Early in his career Galen served as physician to the gladiators of the High Priest of Asia, studying their diet, fitness and living anatomy. Through his work with the gladiators he developed an advanced understanding of physical fitness and training, with which he authored a guide in his 'De Sanitate Tuenda'. Galen divided strength, speed and power training into three categories which he termed: 'strong', 'rapid' and 'violent'.

Strong:
1. Digging
2. Picking up something heavy
3. Picking up something heavy and walking with it
4. Walking uphill
5. Climbing a rope using the hands and feet (commonly along grapplers)
6. Hanging from a rope or beam
7. Holding the arms straight out in front
8. Holding the arms straight out to sides
9. Holding out the arms while a partner pulls them down
10. All three previous exercises while holding something heavy such as jumping weights
11. Breaking loose from a wrestling waist lock
12. Holding onto a person trying to escape from a waist lock

13. Picking up a man who is bending over at the hips and lifting him up and swinging him around
14. Doing the same but bending oneself at the hips also when picking him up
15. Pushing chest to chest trying to force the opponent backwards
16. Hanging from another's neck, attempting to drag him down

Exercises requiring a wrestling pit:
1. Entwine your partner with both your legs around one of his and try to apply a choke or force his head backwards.
2. The same but using only one leg to entwine the opponent's leg closest to yours.
3. The same but using both legs to entwine both of the opponents legs.

Rapid:
1. Running
2. Shadowboxing
3. Boxing
4. Hitting punching bags
5. Throwing and catching a small ball while running
6. Running back and forth, reducing the length each time until finished
7. Stand on the balls of the feet, put the arms up in the air and rapidly and alternately bringing them forward and back; stand near a wall if afraid of losing one's balance
8. Rolling on the wrestling ground rapidly by oneself or with others
9. Rapidly changing places with people next to one in a tightly packed group
10. Jumping up and kicking both legs together backwards
11. Kicking the legs forward alternately
12. Move the arms up and down rapidly with open or closed fist, increasing in speed

Violent:

1. Digging rapidly
2. Casting the discus
3. Jumping repeatedly with no rest
4. Throwing heavy spears and moving fast while wearing heavy armour.
5. Any of the 'strong' exercises executed rapidly: presumably running uphill, swinging jumping weights forward and back, and lifting them up and down, chinups and so on.

Other Exercises:
1. Walking
2. Bending up and down repeatedly at the hips (Good Morning)
3. Lifting a weight up from the ground (Deadlift)
4. Holding up an object for a long time
5. Full and loud breathing (Breathwork)
6. Placing two weights on the ground approximately six feet from each other, picking up the one on the left with the right hand and then the one on the right with the left hand, then in turn placing them back where they came from on the ground and doing this many times with the feet stationary.

Diet:
Barley was the primary carbohydrate source utilized by gladiators (the Latin term for gladiator was 'hordearii', which literally means "barley eaters"), however Galen personally believed the best form of carbohydrates for an athlete was beans, which were commonly used to bulk up gladiators. When talking of beans, Galen says, "there is also much use made of these, since soups are prepared from them, the fluid one in pots and the thick one in pans. Our gladiators eat a great deal of this food every day, making the condition of their body fleshy – not compact, dense flesh like pork, but flesh that is somehow more flabby. The food is flatulent, even if it has been cooked for a very long time, and however it has been prepared, while ptisane gets rid of all flatulent effects during the period of cooking."

Dried fruit was another common source of carbohydrates for gladiators. Additionally, Galen was one of the first people in history to recommend supplementing with whey protein, and his work with gladiators led him to believe that the best protein source was actually pork.

Note: Gladiators were not vegetarian. This misreported claim originates with a single study of a gladiator graveyard in Turkey, which has since been largely debunked. Multiple sources from the time reference fish and pork as common protein sources, however Gladiator schools existed from Britain to Asia, and their diets would've varied from region to region based on what was available.

A strength training program built using real gladiatorial training methods recovered from archeology, Galen and other ancient texts can be found here: https://wildhuntconditioning.myshopify.com/products/gladiator

4. Wrestlers Of Ancient India

As with virtually every other culture on the planet, wrestling was the first martial art practiced in India. Professional grapplers were held in high esteem, with wrestling competitions taking place across all social spheres. A wrestler could even save an entire nation from war by taking part in a deathmatch to settle disputes for the kings as an alternative to conventional warfare between armies of thousands.

Matches were frequently large affairs of great cultural or political significance and could be sponsored by noble or royal houses, and grapplers' training reflected this. It was common for wrestlers to reside together in a training hall, living in a manner often compared to Hindu or Buddhist holy men. Considered extensions of Hanuman, wrestlers were required to remain pure in order to access their highest level of strength and potential. This meant abstaining from smoking, drinking and womanizing to minimize distraction in cultivating themselves into the highest physical, mental and spiritual form possible. Additionally they lived a minimalist existence, their only belongings being a loincloth and a blanket. As often seen, wrestling and strength training shared an intimate relationship, with many grapplers becoming accomplished strongmen (like preenlightenment Buddha and The Great Gama). Feats of strength and wrestling even shared the same patron god, Hanuman.

Training:

•Rangasrama: wrestling and its techniques (submission holds, takedowns and strikes).

•Bodyweight training: baithaks (squats), dands (pushups) and yoga poses.

•Vyayam: General Physical Preparedness (rope climbing, log pulling, running and swimming).

•Pramada: Exercises performed with the gada (stone mace) or weighted club.

•Gonitaka: Exercises done with a large stone ring called a 'gar nal'. It could be swung, lifted or worn around the neck, much like a Bulgarian bag.

•Mallakhamba': the wrestler's pillar, a pillar that was climbed, mounted and dismounted, not unlike a giant stripper pole.

A traditional grappler's khurak (diet) frequently consisted of massive amounts of milk, ghee, almonds with fruit (often dried), chickpeas and green vegetables. Any food that was not prepared by the wrestler (or his family) or was considered excessively sour or spicy were to be avoided. On top of the massive quantities of food he ate, the legendary Indian wrestler and strongman known as the Great Gama also drank 7.5 liters of milk and a mixture made of fruit juice and 1.5 lbs. of crushed almonds every day.

What follows is a story from the book "The Great Gama: The Legendary Wrestler Who Inspired Bruce Lee":

"In 1890, over 400 bodybuilders gathered at the national physical exercise competition of the Rajah of Jodhpur. All at once, they started performing free squats known as baithaks. Sometimes called the Hindu Squat, it's a variant of the regular squat exercise, where you swing your arms to the rhythm of your motion. A standard regimen involves doing one hundred or more of these. At the Raja's contests, grown men performed thousands of these squats for hours on end. One by one, they dropped out due to fatigue. By the time there were just 15 athletes remaining, the Raja called off the contest. It was clear that one of them had earned both the crowd's attention and the prize of the contest – ten year old Mian Ghulam Muhammad. Ghulam would later be bedridden for weeks. But his legendary training regimen is just one of the reasons the Punjabi lion went undefeated in wrestling for 50 years, under the name 'The Great Gama'."

5. Ancient China

China has a history of strength training going back over 5,000 years. It was said that the Yellow Emperor lived to be 113 years old due to his attention to fitness and the great general Tao Kan, who lived to be 76 years old, would move a pile of bricks across his courtyard every morning and then move it back again in the evening. The earliest evidence of calisthenics comes from China and dates back more than 5,000 years, with bodyweight exercises becoming part of military training not long after and organized group calisthenics showing up by the Tang Dynasty (618907 AD). In particular, China was host to a wide variety of functional strength methods. As with most cultures, stone lifting was common in prehistoric China. Eventually the weights shifted to Dings: large bronze cauldrons weighing hundreds of pounds that were used to store and cook food, or make offerings to gods or ancestors. Valued much like the hearth is in many northern cultures, the Ding was associated with sustenance, prosperity, home and family. As such, much ceremonial importance was placed on the activity of Ding lifting and feats of strength were widely celebrated.

Other training methods included:

•Blocks of stone referred to as 'stone locks', which were lifted, swung and thrown in the same manner as kettlebells.

•Large iron bars known as 'Qiaoguan, used as locking bars on doors, were lifted and used for weighted carries, swings and holds.

•Wooden barbells, complete with stone wheels as plates, were in use by the Ming Dynasty.

•Shaolin Monks began every day by bear crawling up and down the steps of their temple.

•Rucking in full kit and armor.

•Carrying or dragging a weighted iron dummy.

•Swinging massive weighted swords and drawing bows with impractically heavy draw weights.

6. Irish Collar And Elbow Wrestling

Collar and Elbow, or "Coiléar agus Uille", is the national wrestling style of Ireland. Historically popular throughout nations with large Irish populations such as Ireland, the United States, Australia and the United Kingdom, it is a form of grappling utilizing fixed grips on jackets and focusing on leg techniques such as trips (referred to as 'hooks'), sweeps, hip throws and in the past even low kicks. Were the modern observer to imagine a judo match in which opponents utilized fixed grips with the right hand on the collar and the left hand gripping the jacket at the elbow, they would not be too far off.

Early matches were often extremely violent as opponents utilized highly kinetic takedowns and fought wearing work boots, resulting in lacerations and broken bones from kicks to the legs. Irish wrestling matches were even known to result in death upon occasion, as demonstrated in an 1888 contest in Killarney when a man died after having his leg broken (in cases like these there appears to have been little to no legal ramifications). Victory was attained by forcing a "fall", the definition of which varied from place to place. In Kildare a fall was defined by making the opponent touch the ground with any part of his body above the knees while in Dublin three points of contact were required to touch the ground (usually both shoulders and a hip or both hips and a shoulder). Other variations in the rules existed as well, such the use of low kicks in Ireland but not in many other countries.

While Collar and Elbow wrestling has declined in popularity throughout much of the Irish diaspora, in the past matches between champions could draw thousands of people from surrounding counties and the art is intricately intertwined in the lore and history of Ireland and its people. US President George Washington was a Collar and Elbow champion, having won the Virginia Collar and Elbow Wrestling Championship at just 18 years old.

7. Wixárika Peyote Pilgrimage

Every year, a small group of members from the Wixárika tribe of northern Mexico travel nearly 500 miles on a pilgrimage to forage for peyote in a place they call Wirikuta, the spiritual homeland where they believe the Sun first emerged, from their home in the remote mountains they retreated to when the Spanish Conquistadors arrived centuries ago. Residing in the remote Sierra Occidental mountains, the Wixáritari live in isolation from the modern world. They speak their own language and raise corn, beans, tomatoes, chilis and livestock in a landscape of vertical rock faces and steep cliffs dotted with cactus and pine, living much like they did before the arrival of the Spanish. The pilgrimage is a link to their ancient past, and a way to both honor their ancestors, preserve their way of life and bring about personal transformation for the small group who undertake the daunting journey.

Before undertaking the journey, the group of travelers must follow a specific ritual. This begins with a cleansing ceremony (part of which is confiding a list of all previous romantic partners) and continues along the route as they stop at sacred desert springs to bless one another and collect branches from a tree they call "raiz amarillo", with which they create a yellow pigment used to paint tiny suns on their cheeks using blades of grass. Once they arrive, the Wixárika sing, dance and play music around the fire through the night. They then take a brief rest before preparing their machetes, baskets and offerings, and heading out to forage for peyote at dawn.

As the sun sets the Wixáritari climb a nearby hill to conduct a ceremony that blesses and cleans their harvest, at which point they each take a microdose (usually just a few bulbs). The pilgrims then leave offerings on the hill before beginning the long journey home. The pilgrimage is considered vital to the survival of the tribe, and failing to perform it correctly is believed to bring calamities like drought, famine or plague. As such a great deal of responsibility rests upon the shoulders of the small group of pilgrims making the nearly 500 mile journey on foot.

8. The Bajau

Having lived entirely at sea for over 1,000 years, the Bajau people have developed genetic variations that make them the best divers and swimmers on the planet. Maritime nomads who roam the South Pacific live on small boats that they tie together into floating villages. The Bajau are a peaceful people who find sustenance by using their freediving skills to hunt, fish and gather food and materials for trade from the ocean's depths. Scientists credit intense natural selection for the unique genetic variations that lead to the improved underwater adaptations seen amongst the Bajau.

For example, while worldclass free divers in the modern world can hold their breath for up to 34 minutes, Bajau divers have been observed to easily hold their breath for 5 minutes or more on routine dives. Bajau swimmers have also been observed diving down to depths of over 200 feet with only a weight belt and a pair of wooden goggles, both homemade. Some are even said to intentionally burst their eardrums in their youth, enabling them to reach even greater depths but leaving them deaf in old age. Bajau spleens are about 50 percent larger, storing more haemoglobin rich blood, allowing them to hold their breath much longer than other humans. Additionally, other genetic variations have been detected amongst the Bajau including variations responsible for resistance to the effects of oxygen deprivation and carbon dioxide accumulation as well as one granting improved underwater vision. Another identified gene variation affects the 'diving response', a set of physiological responses to underwater immersion that restricts blood from the limbs and organs to preserve blood and oxygen for the heart, brain and lungs.

No one knows where they come from, but some of the Bajau have a legend which tells that they were once elite bodyguards to a mighty empire. After failing to protect their princess on a sea journey they refused to return home, choosing instead to roam the ocean eternally in penance.

PEOPLE

9. Rocky Marciano

Rocco Francis Marchegiano was born to Italian immigrants on the south side of Brockton, Massachusetts in September of 1923. His early years were difficult and at 18 months old he contracted a severe case of pneumonia that nearly killed him. As a boy, "Rocky" built a homemade weightlifting set up and began using a stuffed mailbag hung from a tree in his backyard as a heavy bag. He used both as tools to develop his strength and endurance to great effect. After 10th grade, Marciano dropped out of school and went to work as a chute man, later working as a ditch digger and railroad layer as well. In 1943 he was drafted into the US Army, and shortly before his discharge Marciano won the 1946 Amateur Armed Forces boxing tournament.

Turning pro in 1948, Rocky did not appear to be imposing for his weight class. Standing 5'10" and weighing between 185 lbs. and 205 lbs. throughout his career, he was a small heavyweight with short arms who lacked the technical boxing skills seen at the professional level. However it soon became clear that Marciano had unbreakable heart, unstoppable conditioning, tremendous durability and devastating knockout power. He worked his way into close range and made fights dirty, overwhelming opponents with the volume and power of his punches, until he won the title from Jersey Joe Walcott on September 23, 1952. Rocky would go on to finish his career 4900 with 43 wins by knockout. Boxing historians described his right hand as the most devastating weapon ever brought into the ring.

Marciano believed endurance was his biggest weapon and was completely devoted to being the best conditioned boxer alive. He ran 5 miles every day of his life, and 12 miles per day during fight camps, even if “it was pouring rain or Christmas morning”. He trained strength with physical culture icon Charles Atlas, shadowboxed for hours in neck deep water and did pushups, sit ups and chin ups until his coach forced him to stop (at which point he would do 100 more). His brother Peter said Rocky lived like a monk, was totally devoted to training and being able to throw more punches than he would ever face. His pressure and stamina were so relentless that Archie Moore said fighting him was like fighting an airplane propeller. Further, when asked about Rocky’s strength, Moore said, “He was the strongest man, bar none, that I ever met in the ring. And I fought some strong men.”

His diet consisted of primarily rare red meat and vegetables, mostly steak but also lamb, veal, and a little chicken from time to time, with baked potatoes, green vegetables and a salad with oil and vinegar dressing. He drank skim milk, turnip juice and tea, and carried a jar of honey around with him.

In addition to being one of the most dedicated men to ever set foot in the ring, Marciano remains the only fighter in history to have stopped every opponent he faced for a world heavyweight title.

A training plan based on the historical training methods of Rocky, Muhammad Ali, Mike Tyson and many others can be found here:

https://wildhuntconditioning.myshopify.com/products/oldschoolfighter

10. Rickson Gracie

Rickson Gracie is said to be the best Brazilian Jiu Jitsu practitioner of all time and was widely considered to be the Gracie clan's strongest fighter. One of legendary BJJ pioneer Helio Gracie's nine sons, he represented the Gracie family during a time when the martial arts world was wild and untamed. Clashes between opposing disciplines and schools were commonplace, and frequently devolved into brawls and riots. In the past, the Gracies had issued an open challenge for martial artists from competing styles to try their luck in challenge fights. In response, fighters from disciplines like wrestling, boxing, karate, kickboxing and Capoeira arrived from all over the world to challenge the Gracie Clan.

None were known to make it past Rickson.

Rickson's style was that of a sleek predator, and this extended beyond just his jiu jitsu. Whereas most fighters trained to be elite athletes, or trained like tough guys, Rickson trained to be an apex hunter. He embraced a diverse set of natural training methods consistent with a man that many associated more with a lion:

•As seen in historic boxers and hardened inmates, old school fighters often focused on bodyweight training and Rickson was no different. In addition to a wide variety of basic calisthenics movements, he also worked extensively on movement through gymnastics, yoga and simulating the movement patterns of animals. Push ups, pull ups, squats, dips, underwater exercise, core work, rings, bars, beams, ropes and poles all played a part in his strength routine. He was also an early pioneer of training with resistance bands, making his own from the rubber tubing of a speargun.

Training notes:

•He practiced breath work daily, and was known to use this skill to battle fatigue and anxiety during fights. He became legendary for his mental and respiratory control, and has since written a book on the topic.

•Rickson surfed, hiked or rode his bike daily to build endurance and promote active recovery. Before fights in Japan, he would hike deep into the mountains and do breath work in a freezing stream.

•When preparing for a fight he lifted weights and began to embrace longer rest periods, allowing him to achieve higher levels of training intensity.

•His neck was so strong he could pull a car uphill by a rope attached to his head.

Diet:
Rickson adhered to the 'Gracie Diet', a diet based on food combinations:
Group A- Animal protein, fats, oils and vegetables.
Group B- Cereals.
Group C- Sweet fruits.
Group D- Acidic fruits.

•Gracie Diet guidelines:
Foods from group A combine with each other and with one of group B.
Foods from group C combine with each other and with one of group B.
Foods from group B do not combine with each other.
Foods from group D can only be consumed individually.
Avoid pork, alcohol and smoking.

Meals:
•Breakfast: coffee, whole grain bread and white cheese.

•Morning snack: fruit smoothie with protein powder and vitamin.

•Lunch: plate of green leaves with cashews, boiled vegetables, brown rice and chicken breast.

•Afternoon snack: frozen açaí pulp, papaya, dates and granola.

•Evening snack: baked pastry stuffed with ricotta cheese and a glass of beet juice.

•Dinner: 2 eggs, 5 egg whites and a sweet potato.

•Supper: whole grain bread, white cheese.

•Night Snack: chopped oranges.

11. Babe Ruth

Babe Ruth was known to eat ten hotdogs in a sitting, sleep with six women at a time, chain smoke cigars and gamble huge sums of money. He was given to excess with both food and alcohol, with his husky frame measuring 6’2” 260 lbs. He began playing baseball in juvenile hall rather than a fancy school, and was commonly described as both sloppy and ugly. Not exactly the picture of modern fitness. And yet to this day he is considered by some to be the best baseball player of all time, while none can deny his incredible slugging power and status as an American icon.

However by 1925, Babe’s lifestyle had begun to catch up with him. Overweight, unhappy and in a slump, he started training like a madman. He hired trainer Artie McGovern, a former flyweight boxer who provided strength and conditioning to top athletes of the day including Jack Dempsey. McGovern, called the "Father of Fitness," approaches training with intelligence and precision, putting his athletes through rigorous training sessions and monitoring their diets closely. McGovern dismissed quick fixes and fad diets, favoring balanced nutrition, weight training, stretching and cardio. He utilized a well rounded approach that focused on functional strength, sports specific training and the targeting of muscles not developed by the sport itself. McGovern insisted all his clients learn boxing and wrestling for conditioning (even Opera singers and the wives of millionaires) and required them all to spar, something Ruth enjoyed thoroughly.

Ruth would return for the 1926 season a changed man, hitting three home runs in a single World Series game and leading a team so skilled they were referred to as 'Murderer's Row'.

Diet:

•Breakfast Porterhouse Steak, Potatoes, Quart of Bourbon and Ginger Ale, 18 Egg Omelette
•Snack #1 2 Hot Dogs, 2 CocaCola
•Lunch 2 Raw Steak, 2 Orders Potatoes, 1 Lettuce Head with Roquefort Dressing
•Snack #2 2 Hot Dogs, 2 CocaCola
•Dinner 2 Porterhouse Steaks raw, 2 Lettuce Heads with roquefort dressing, 2 Cottage Fried Potatoes, 2 order of Apple Pie
•After Dinner Snack Chocolate Ice Cream, Picked Eels

Calories: 9,159
Protein: 519
Carbohydrates: 504
Fat: 422

Bonus:

Babe Ruth's Ab Workout:

In the 1926 World Series, Babe Ruth hit three home runs in one game. His trainer would say, "I believe the intensive abdominal workouts we gave Babe in 1925 were as much responsible for the great showing he made during the 1926 season."

Exercise 1: Weighted Vacuum (40 reps)
1. Lie face up in a classic situp position. Hold a book or weight against your abdomen.
2. Raise the weight by expanding your abdomen, then lower it by relaxing your stomach.

Exercise 2: Supine Alternating Toe Touches (6 reps for each side)
1. Lie faceup with your arms and legs extended.
2. Keeping your arms and legs straight, lift your right arm and left leg up, trying to touch your left toes with your right hand.
3. Return to start and repeat on the other side.

Exercise 3: Reverse Supine Alternating Toe Touches (6 reps for each side)
1. Reverse exercise 2: Start with your arms and legs lifted up as if you were trying to touch your toes.
2. Lower your left leg and right arm simultaneously, keeping your right leg and left arm lifted.
3. Return to the top and lower the right leg and left arm. Alternate.

Exercise 4: V-Up and Touch (6 reps)
1. McGovern calls this the "perfect abdominal exercise." Lie faceup with arms and legs fully extended.
2. Keeping both your arms and legs straight, raise your legs until they are perpendicular with your torso so your feet point at the ceiling. At the same time, raise your arms up and to the sides of your legs until your palms touch the floor next to your butt.
3. Return to start.

Exercise 5: Straight Leg SitUp (6 reps)
1. Lie faceup with your arms and legs extended.
2. Keeping your legs on the ground, perform a sit up, reaching for your toes.

Exercise 6: Arm and Leg Clap (6 reps)
1. Lie faceup with your arms extended straight in front of your chest, and your legs perpendicular to the floor so that your feet point toward the ceiling.
2. Place your hands together and your feet together.
3. Now simultaneously separate your arms and legs so both form "V" shapes.
4. Clap them back together.

Exercise 7: Arm and Leg Scissor (8 reps for each side)
1. Start in the same position as exercise 6, with hands touching each other and feet touching each other.
2. This time, cross your legs and arms simultaneously to one side, return to start, then cross the other way.

12. Muhammad Ali

Named after his father, who was himself named after a 19th century Republican Abolitionist, Cassius Marcellus Clay Jr. was born in Louisville in 1942. Of African and Irish ancestry, Ali grew up during an era of racial segregation, something that would impact him deeply. He was first introduced to boxing by a Louisville police officer named Joe E. Martin when he was 12 years old, after his bicycle was stolen. Ali told Officer Martin he was going to "whup" the thief. Martin then told him he had better learn how to box first. In addition to being a police officer, Martin was also a boxing coach and one of the early civil rights activists in Louisville, with one of the only racially integrated gyms in the city. Martin would take Ali under his wing and go on to coach him through six Kentucky Golden Gloves titles, two national Golden Gloves titles and a gold medal in the 1960 Olympics in Rome.

Ali would go on to win the World Heavyweight Champion at age 22 and be declared by many to be the greatest boxer of all time, with wins over Sonny Liston, Joe Frazier, George Foreman and Floyd Patterson.

Ali was known widely for his dedication to training, even building his own compound in Deer Lake, Pennsylvania, and calling it "Fighter's Heaven". Training in the compound was highly disciplined, including a daily 4:30AM wakeup to run 6 miles and chop wood before breakfast (poached eggs, wheat toast and grapefruit juice) and multiple boxing sessions throughout the day. Ali took strength and conditioning seriously, but like many old school boxers he did not lift weights, instead relying on chopping wood, running hills, calisthenics, jumping rope and shadowboxing. He famously said that he didn't even count reps until it started to burn, and was known for the amazing number of sit up and crunch variations he was capable of. In his prime Muhammad Ali was one of the best conditioned athletes on the planet.

Fun fact: chopping wood with an axe was Ali's favorite form of physical conditioning, and he used to say it was the perfect way to get ready to cut down men in the ring.

13. Walt Whitman

American Poet Walt Whitman believed that life was a fight and that one had to build in themselves a "solid and adamantine fiber which would endure long and serious attacks". To this end, he woke early everyday to do calisthenics for one hour, swim in a cold river and then eat a plate of unflavored lean meat with a chunk of bread and a cup of tea. In the evening, he wrestled a twelve foot oak tree for exercise every night well into his 60's, even after suffering a stroke. His daily calisthenics routine was always performed outdoors, and was as follows:

WARMUP
Dynamic Overhead Stretch (10 reps)
Whitman's instructions: "Throw forward the arms, with vigorous motion, and then extend them or lift them upward."

Active Plank (8 reps)
Whitman's instructions: "Place the body in position occasionally, for a moment, with all the sinews of the arms and legs strained to their utmost tension."

Lunges (8 reps for each side)
Whitman's instructions: "Take very long strides rapidly forward,

and then, more slowly and carefully, backward."

Single Leg Deadlift (4 reps for each side)
Whitman's instructions: "The simple exercise of standing on one foot and lowering so as to touch the bent knee of the other leg to the ground, and then rising again on the first foot, is also a good one."

Fence or Bench Hops (10 reps for 4 sets)
Whitman's instructions: ". . . spring over a fence, and then back again, and then again and again . . ."

Shadowboxing (4 rounds)
Whitman's instructions: ". . . pummel some imaginary foe, with stroke after stroke from the doubled fists, given with a will . . ."

Jump Squats (number of reps varies)
Whitman's instructions: ". . . clap the palms of the hands on the hips and simply jump straight up, two or three minutes at a time . . ."

"There was a contest, called the Pancratium, which included all means of defense and offense, at the option of the fighter, who was expected to do the best he could for himself, and the worst for his adversary. It was lawful to scratch, bite, gouge, kickin short, just like a modern Arkansas rough and tumble of the severest kind, barring the bowie knife. These games, in which all were interested and most of the young and middle aged men partook, served to make a very hardy and handsome bodied race. In such severe exercises, the Greeks not only prepared themselves for the hardships and contests of war, but for the enjoyment of life, and to acquire a happy and vigorous national temper."

Walt Whitman, 1858

14. Bernard Hopkins

At 49 years old, Bernard Hopkins would become the oldest boxer in history to win a world title. This was the culmination of a historic career that included multiple championship titles and victories over some of the best boxers in history, including a win over Oscar De La Hoya that made him the first male boxer ever to simultaneously hold world titles by all four major boxing sanctioning bodies.

When he was 17 years old Hopkins was incarcerated in Graterford Prison for committing nine felonies, having already been stabbed three times. After witnessing the murder of another inmate over a pack of cigarettes, Hopkins decided to change his life. He began boxing and spent the rest of his sentence developing the monklike focus and pugilistic skills that would define him. By the time of his release, he had compiled a prison boxing record of 95 wins and 4 losses.

Later in life, Hopkins would attribute his personal discipline to his experiences and time spent in prison. This discipline reigned in all areas of Bernard's life. He abstained from drugs, alcohol, smoking, processed food and staying up late. He cooked his own meals with fresh ingredients, organic produce and whole grains purchased every day or two, and has joked that he's the one who made Trader Joe rich. Venison was his primary protein source (he has a special butcher outside Philadelphia who prepares the meat and organs for him), though he also favored bison. Altogether, far more variety than the peanut butter sandwiches he survived on as a teenage prison boxer.

Like many old school boxers Hopkins did not
lift weights, saying lifting weights "makes you look good, but you are not walking the beach. In the ring you need to be mobile, flexible and quick". Believing that the best resistance was your own body, he focused on calisthenics, running, stretching and coordination. He played chess and did puzzles to train his mind, and even carried a tennis ball with him to bounce and dribble to

further build his reflexes.

“I am an old man, I just happen to be an old man who can fight.” Bernard Hopkins

Weekly Routine:
•Monday Run (30 mins), Stretch (40 mins) and Boxing, including jump rope (90 mins).

•Tuesday Run (60 mins), Watch Tape, Stretch (40 mins) and Boxing, including speed bag (90 mins).

•Wednesday Run (30 mins), Stretch (40 mins) and Boxing, including pads and heavy bag (90 mins).

•Thursday Run (sprints), Stretch (40 mins) and Boxing, including sparring (90 mins).

•Friday Run (60 mins), Massage, Stretch (40 mins) and Boxing, including heavy bag and jumping rope (90 mins).

•Saturday Rest.

•Sunday Rest.

15. Aleksandr Karelin

Aleksandr Karelin is widely considered by many to be not only the greatest wrestler of all time, but the strongest. Competing for the Soviet Union, he would win gold in three Olympics and nine world championships. Weighing over 12 lbs. at birth, by the time he started wrestling at age thirteen he was 5’10” and 174 lbs and was already stronger than grown men his size. Karelin grew and matured extremely fast, reaching his full stature of 6’3” and 286 lbs. within a few years.

In addition to his unmatched grappling skill, Karelin was known for his legendary strength, which earned him the nickname of "The Experiment". Despite weighing nearly 300 lbs. he was able to do a backflip, the splits or 42 pull ups. His conditioning sessions lasted hours, favoring hard rowing or long runs through frozen boreal forests with a large log on his back. Every day he did overhead presses with a 71 lbs. kettlebell and carried his refrigerator in a bear hug up the eight flights of stairs leading to his apartment. His unusual physiology and training style allowed Karelin to clean and press 420 lbs., bench press 450 lbs. and Zercher deadlift 440 lbs. ten times. He even took part in the 1991 European Hercules Strongman Competition, managing to place 8th.

Karelin would become infamous for the 'Karelin Lift', a throw rarely used by heavyweights because of the immense strength required to raise, spin and slam the nearly 600 lbs. combined weight of both athletes (half of which would be resisting violently).

"He didn't just dominate the world of Greco-Roman wrestling, for 13 years, he terrified the world of Greco-Roman wrestling!"

16. Charles Bronson

Charles Bronson was a kind and bright boy known for defending weaker children from bullies. As he got older it became clear that he was comfortable with violence and loved to fight, and by age 13 he was part of a robbery gang. His first job was at a grocery store, however he was fired after two weeks for attacking his manager. He would spend much of his life incarcerated for armed robbery, during which he developed a savage reputation for attacks on other inmates, including strangling a pedophile and attacking an inmate who informed on his escape plan, permanently scarring the man, among many others. Moved to solitary confinement, Bronson became obsessed with physical fitness.

Much like Muhammad Ali, Rickson Gracie and Mike Tyson, Bronson favored calisthenics training for the athletic and functional benefits, believing a focus on health, fitness and stamina was the secret to being lean and dangerous, rather than excess muscle mass (once during a short stint on the outside, Bronson almost beat up two men at a local gym for asking how big his biceps were). Despite his focus on training with only his own body weight, he was still unnaturally strong, able to do 25 push ups with two men on his back or lift a pool table. Once, despite not training with weights for eight years, he was still able to bench press 300 lbs. for ten reps and at his peak he was said to put up 500 for a single rep. He valued functional strength and had little use for aesthetic mass, pointing out that big biceps actually reduced punching power (a statement backed by many professional boxers).

Countless prison fights, acts of street violence and an illegal bare knuckle boxing career had taught him that appearance mattered little, but ability mattered a lot. Bronson's favorite exercises were handstand push ups, squats, dips, sit ups and burpees. He believed in an extensive warm up, good sleep, regular stretching and that a man trained best "after a crap".

Like Bronson, I also started my physical training journey while incarcerated. Anyone who is interested can find my entire training plan here:

https://wildhuntconditioning.myshopify.com/products/thedubmethod

17. Abraham Lincoln

Before Abraham Lincoln was the 16th President of the United States of America, he was a lawyer. Many know this. What they don't know is that before Abe was a lawyer, he was a mixed martial arts fighter. Growing up in the frontier town of New Salem, Lincoln was known for three things: his love of reading, his immense physical strength and his grappling ability. One of the best fighters around, the 6'4" and 185 lbs. Lincoln practiced what was known as Frontier Wrestling, similar to Catch Wrestling, which included joint locks, pins and even strikes, depending on the rules of the match. He won the Illinois County wrestling championship in 1830 and store clerk Bill Green claimed Lincoln could "outrun, outfit, out wrestle and throw down any man in Sangamon County" after watching him fight a gang of newcomers in 1831.

Lincoln would become a figure of frontier legend for his street fight with Jack Armstrong, the leader of a gang called the Clary's Grove Boys, who liked to nail people inside barrels and toss them off hills. The people of his hometown, tired of being terrorized, began asking the introverted Lincoln to "take care" of Armstrong. Upon hearing this, the boisterous Armstrong sought out Lincoln and challenged him first. The story goes that both men were skilled fighters and neither could initially gain an advantage. Over time Lincoln would wear him down and, becoming enraged when his opponent attempted a dirty move, knocked Armstrong out cold with a slam.

Abraham Lincoln would finish his career with a record of 3001, his sole loss coming from a match with a fellow soldier while serving as a captain in the Illinois Volunteers during the Black Hawk War, and was inducted into the National Wrestling Hall of Fame.

18. George Washington

Known throughout his life for his physical strength, George Washington was a physical renaissance man who attained a high degree of skill in most of the sports of his day. He practiced archery, hunting, wrestling, sword fighting and swimming, and according to Thomas Jefferson, Washington was the best horseman of their age. At just 18 years old, he won the highly competitive Virginia Collar and Elbow Wrestling Championship. Lacking any formal education, he spent his teen years surveying the backwoods and by the time he won a Collar and Elbow wrestling championship in Virginia at age 18, he was already famed for his physical strength, hardiness and grappling skill.

One day in 1773, several men were competing at Mount Vernon to see who could throw an iron bar the farthest. Suddenly Washington appeared and politely asked to try. His attempt was described by one of the men present: "no sooner...did that heavy iron bar feel the grasp of his mighty hand than it lost the power of gravitation and whizzed through the air, striking the ground far, very far, beyond our utmost limits."

Washington maintained a high level of fitness throughout his entire life, and at the age of 47 he was still able to defeat seven consecutive challengers from the Massachusetts Volunteers in wrestling matches.

19. Bruce Lee

Born in San Francisco in 1940 to a Chinese father and a ChineseBritish mother, Bruce Lee requires little introduction. A legendary martial artist and student of physical culture, he was voted one of 100 most important people of the 20th century by TIME Magazine. His public persona influenced generations of men and helped bridge the gap between east and west, but it was his private training, study and innovation that truly defined the man.

Lee's martial arts experience began with street fighting, boxing and Wing Chun (including training under the legendary Ip Man), coming up in Hong Kong during a lawless era where soaring crime and minimal police presence saw large-scale gang violence.

In order to avoid crackdowns by the British Hong Kong police, gangs and rival martial arts schools would meet on rooftops to challenge each other to bare knuckle fights, often inflicting savage beatings. This violent and unforgiving climate was hard on young men, but it was particularly difficult for Bruce, his mixed ancestry preventing him from training at most martial arts schools and making him a target among the ethnic Chinese of Hong Kong.

Moving to America, the country of his birth, Bruce would become fascinated with the melting pot of American martial arts and physical culture. He became particularly interested in grappling, strength training and nutrition. A true student of the martial arts, Bruce trained judo and catch wrestling under Gene Lebell, picked up boxing footwork from Muhammad Ali, learned kicks from Taekowndo Grandmaster Rhee Jhoongoo and studied the functional grappling strength methods of the Great Gama. He would combine all of these influences and lessons to establish his own style of martial arts, Jeet Kune Do, with many considering the style a forebearer to modern mixed martial arts. Several of the techniques Bruce was known for have since proven highly effective in the highest levels of MMA completion, such as the oblique kick to manage distance and hyperextend the knee or the calf kick, which can quickly shut down the leg or even break the bone.

In addition to being a true student of the martial arts, Bruce was also known for his unmatched physical fitness. Lee felt that it was a huge mistake to overlook physical training, as most of the martial artists of his day did, and that the development of the individual was necessary in addition to the development of the skill. As with his martial arts training, Bruce was decades ahead of his time: he utilized functional strength training, traditional bodybuilding, dynamic effort training (moving moderate weights with explosive speed), running, isometrics, high intensity interval training and sports specific exercises, all still utilized today at the highest levels of athletics and combat training. He also tried experimental technologies new at the time, such as electric muscle stimulation and complex resistance machines. His emphasis on strength of the back, core and grip, using compound lifts to move moderate weights with explosive speed, utilizing bodybuilding accessories to armor and build the body and placing great focus on conditioning all echo the wisdom of powerlifting legend Louie Simmons and his elite strength gym, Westside Barbell, who hold countless world records and remain at the cutting edge of strength training to this day.

While there are many legends surrounding the physical feats he accomplished, some have been confirmed including doing push ups with only his index finger and thumb, training with a 300 lbs. heavy bag, pushing his fingers through the wall of an unopened can of Cola (cans were made from steel at the time) and having strikes too fast to be picked up by the cameras of the day.

Bruce's weekly routine was as follows:

Day 1:
AM:
Clean and Press: 2 x 8-12
Barbell Curls: 2 x 8-12
Behind the Neck Presses: 2 x 8-12
Upright Rows: 2 x 8-12
Barbell Squats: 2 x 12-20
Barbell Row: 2 x 8-12
Bench Press: 2 x 8-12
Barbell Pullover: 2 x 8-12
Sit Ups: 5 x failure
Leg Raises: 5 x failure
Side Bends: 5 x failure

PM:
Martial Arts training.

Day 2:
AM:
Sit Ups: 5 x failure
Leg Raises: 5 x failure
Side Bends: 5 x failure
4 mile run while meditating, variable intensity.

PM:
Martial Arts training.

Day 3:
AM:
Sit Ups: 5 x failure
Leg Raises: 5 x failure
Side Bends: 5 x failure
Clean and Press: 2 x 8-12
Barbell Curls: 2 x 8-12
Behind the Neck Presses: 2 x 8-12
Upright Rows: 2 x 8-12
Barbell Squats: 2 x 12-20
Barbell Row: 2 x 8-12
Bench Press: 2 x 8-12
Barbell Pullover: 2 x 8-12

PM:
Martial Arts training.

Day 4:
AM:
Sit Ups: 5 x failure
Leg Raises: 5 x failure
Side Bends: 5 x failure
4 mile run while meditating, variable intensity.

PM:

Martial Arts training.

Day 5:
AM:
Sit Ups: 5 x failure
Leg Raises: 5 x failure
Side Bends: 5 x failure
Clean and Press: 2 x 8-12
Barbell Curls: 2 x 8-12
Behind the Neck Presses: 2 x 8-12
Upright Rows: 2 x 8-12
Barbell Squats: 2 x 12-20
Barbell Row: 2 x 8-12
Bench Press: 2 x 8-12
Barbell Pullover: 2 x 8-12

PM:
Martial Arts training.

Day 6:
AM:
Sit Ups: 5 x failure
Leg Raises: 5 x failure
Side Bends: 5 x failure
4 mile run while meditating, variable intensity.

PM:
Martial Arts training.

Day 7:
AM:
Martial Arts Training.

-

He would also use the following circuit for conditioning during peak training cycles:

•Pull Up: 30 seconds

•Seated Leg Press: 30 seconds

•Hip/Knee Extensions: 30 seconds

•Shoulder Press: 30 seconds

•Standing Calf Raise: 30 seconds (with varying foot positions)

•Alternating Cable Curl: 30 seconds•Standing Unilateral Arm Adduction: 30 seconds

•Bench Press: 30 seconds

•Conventional Deadlift: 30 seconds

•Kneeling Pulldown Behind Neck: 30 seconds

•Triceps Push Down: 30 seconds

•Sprint: 90 seconds

•Standing Wrist Roller: 1 minute

•Neck Flexion/Extension: 1 minute

Diet:
Bruce's diet was simple. He believed that achieving a high performance body was no different from maintaining the engine of a high performance automobile, both requiring high octane fuel. He avoided refined flour, particularly baked goods, and dairy (instead preferring powdered milk) while preferring a high protein diet rich in vitamins and minerals. A fan of Asian cuisine for its culinary diversity and nutritional variety, he ate a lot of fish, steak, rice and vegetables. He believed in eating organ meats for their nutrient density, favored tea made with ginseng and royal jelly and had a secret protein shake recipe, listed here:

- Protein powder
- Eggs
- Powdered milk
- Wheat germ
- Peanut butter
- Bananas
- Brewers' yeast
- Inositol
- Granular lecithin

Bruce's training methods have stood the test of time incredibly well, from his martial arts to his strength training to his nutrition, proof of the power of having an open, studious mind and complete dedication to your craft.

20. John Colter

John Colter was born in the Colony of Virginia in 1774. Widely considered America's first mountain man, the outdoor skills he had developed from this frontier lifestyle impressed Meriwether Lewis so much that he offered Colter the rank of Private plus five dollars per month to join the Lewis and Clark Expedition. Colter was disciplined at different points, once for leaving camp to go to a whisky shop north of St. Louis, and again not long after for threatening to shoot his sergeant, however he was also considered the expedition's best woodsman and was given much responsibility. He was often sent out alone to hunt meat and scout the terrain, and was instrumental in the expedition finding passes through the Rocky Mountains. Upon his discharge, Colter was paid a total of $179.33 for his service. He never once appeared in the expedition's sick lists.

A few years after, while leading a group of 800 Flathead and Crow Indians, the party was attacked by 1,500 Blackfeet warriors and

Colter took an arrow to the leg. He would heal, however the next year he would indeed be captured by the Blackfeet, who killed and dismembered his companion and proceeded to beat and strip Colter naked. He was then hunted for sport by their warriors, running for his life naked through the wilderness. After several miles he had outpaced all of his pursuers except one, who began to close on him. Colter suddenly turned and attacked, killing the warrior with the man's own spear. From there he continued on, reaching the Madison river five miles from his start and hiding inside a beaver dam. Emerging after dark, he climbed and successfully walked eleven days to the trader's fort on the Little BigHorn.

21. Hydna

Hydna was born in the Greek coastal city of Scione sometime around 500 BC. Her father, Scyllias, was a highly skilled diver and swim instructor. He trained Hydna throughout her youth and as she matured she began to work alongside him as a diver, helping to earn a living for her family. At the time the whole of Greece lived in fear of Persian invasion, with tensions rising and most believing it would be impossible to turn back the millions of soldiers the Persian king Xerxes could bring to battle. And in 480 BC, Xerxes did indeed invade: crossing the Hellespont into Greece with a massive army, likely the biggest the world had ever seen, which murdered, raped and burned everything in their path. Citystates crumbled, towns were wiped from history and cultures that had been around for centuries were ground out under Persian boots.

Until this army met 300 Spartans in a narrow pass called the Hot Gates. For three days the Spartan king Leonidas and his 300 bodyguards held off the 300,000 man Persian army, killing thousands of the best soldiers from the nations of Asia, before being overrun in a legendary last stand. The example of their sacrifice spread like a wildfire through the hearts of the Greeks, including Hydna and her father, Scyllias.

Prior to the Battle of Artemisium Xerxes had moored his ships off the coast of Mount Pelion to wait out a storm. Despite having no military training or combat experience, that night Hydna and her father swam ten miles through the choppy storm waters with only a dagger each. Upon reaching the Persian fleet, the girl and her father swam silently among the ships cutting their ropes and dragging away their anchors. This resulted in the ships being violently slammed against each other by the storm, with many being damaged or sunk.

Their attack delayed the Persians, giving the Greeks more time to prepare and leading to their eventual victory at the Battle of Salamis. In recognition of the heroism shown by Hydna and her father, the Greeks dedicated statues to them at the most sacred site of the Greek world, Delphi.

22. Harry Haft

Hertzka 'Harry' Haft was born on 28 July 1925 in Bełchatów, Poland. When we was 14 years old his country was invaded and occupied by Nazi Germany. Because he was Jewish, Haft was imprisoned in a concentration camp where he was beaten, starved and used as slave labor. Having taken notice of his strong physique, an SS overseer began training him in boxing. He was then forced to compete in fights to the death for the amusement of German soldiers, which took place at the Jaworzno concentration camp located at a coal mine north of Auschwitz. Over the course of the war Haft would survive a total of 76 of these death matches.

When the Soviet Army began advancing on Jaworzno at the war's end, Haft and his fellow prisoners were sent on a death march. Haft managed to escape. On the run and hunted by the Nazis, Haft managed to kill a German soldier while he bathed and stole his uniform. Wearing the uniform as a disguise, he travelled through enemy territory until he managed to reach a refugee camp run by the United States Army. Haft continued to box, and in 1947 he won the United States Army's Amateur Jewish Heavyweight Championship in Munich.

Immigrating to America, Haft would make his living as a light heavyweight prizefighter with wins in his first 12 fights. In 1949, he knocked Bill Kirby out in the first round with a right cross that broke Kirby's jaw. Five months later he TKO'd Johnny Pretzie, a hard hitter with a bunch of knockouts on his record, in Brooklyn. The final fight of Haft's career would be against the legendary Rocky Marciano, where he hung with Marciano blow for blow through the first two rounds before getting caught by a flurry of Marciano's punches in the third, getting stopped.

After his loss to Marciano in 1949, Haft retired. He married, had children and opened a fruit and vegetable store in Brooklyn. In 2007 he was included in the Jewish Sports Hall of Fame, dying later that year at the age of 82.

23. George Foreman

George Foreman grew up in the Fifth Ward of Houston, Texas as one of seven siblings. A troubled youth, he dropped out of school at the age of 15 to earn money robbing people. A year or two later he got his act together and began working as a bricklayer and carpenter after getting his GED. Soon after he got into boxing, leading to his defeat of the Soviet champion to win a gold medal in the 1968 Olympics in Mexico City.

Turning pro, Foreman quickly became famous as a tough slugger with enormous punching power. Foreman quickly tore through all the competition, earning him a fight with the world heavyweight champion Joe Frazier. In their fight, Foreman would knock down Frazier six times in the first two rounds, finishing him by TKO in the 2nd round and becoming the new world heavyweight champion. Foreman would retire shortly after a loss to Muhammad Ali, and soon after had a religious awakening. He would spend the following years as an ordained minister preaching to the homeless on street corners, before becoming the reverend of a Houston church.

However ten years after his retirement, he would make a comeback. Despite the doubts of commentators and the public alike, in 1994 at age 45 George Foreman became the oldest heavyweight boxing champion in history by winning the unified WBA, IBF and lineal heavyweight championship titles with a knock out of 26 year old Michael Moorer. Foreman said he managed to rise to the top despite being in his mid40's due to his attention to training and nutrition. Like many fighters of his day Foreman preferred bodyweight training and chopping wood to weight lifting, however later he adopted weights and credits them with playing a big role in his comeback.

24. Bob "The Fighting Blacksmith" Fitzsimmons

Born in May of 1863 as one of twelve children, Bob Fitzsimmons was a former blacksmith who would go on to become the first boxer in history to become a three division world champion. Fitzsimmons was one of the hardest punchers in the history of boxing, despite being the smallest heavyweight champion in history at just 5 '11 " and 165 lbs. (he still holds a place in The Guinness Book of World Records as the lightest heavyweight champion in history). The size disparity between him and his larger opponents was such that Fitzsimmons wore heavy wool briefs into the ring in an attempt to look bigger.

After fighting in the amateurs in New Zealand, Fitzsimmons began his professional career in Australia in 1883 where he quickly showed an ability to win fights by knockout. Bob learned his distinctive movement and punching style from an old school bareknuckle boxer named Jem Mace, who taught Fitzsimmons to draw on the power he had developed from his years of hammering and bending hot iron as a blacksmith. Mace helped him harness his incredible power into short, accurate punches that knocked out man after man, with his signature shot being a savage uppercut to the solar plexus. It was not long until the thin and rangy Fitzsimmons became known as the hardest hitter in boxing.

After coming to America and winning the middleweight title, Fitzsimmons began a run at heavyweight that included a fight in San Francisco which was officiated by legendary Wild West lawman Wyatt Earp. This run culminated in a fight with the heavyweight champ Jim Corbett, who had won the title five years earlier by beating John L. Sullivan. The two met in Carson City and it quickly became clear that Corbett was the more skilled boxer, not to mention much larger. He outboxed Fitzsimmons for several rounds, knocking him down in the sixth round and badly damaging his face. However Fitzsimmons kept coming and eventually Corbett began to slow down. In the 14th round, Fitzsimmons managed to land his signature uppercut to the solar plexus and Corbett collapsed in agony, unable to continue. This was the first ever knockout recorded on film.

At 165 lbs., The Fighting Blacksmith was the new world heavyweight champion.

25. Louie Simmons

The original Westside Barbell was created in California in the early 1960's by a man named Bill "Peanuts" West, who started the gym in his garage. Pioneering strange new techniques like the box squat and the board press, West's garage gym would become a home to early powerlifting legends like George Frenn and Pat Casey. Their revolutionary ideas spread throughout the powerlifting world, all the way to Germany where a young American soldier named Louie Simmons read them about in a magazine and took inspiration. Returning home to Columbus, Ohio, Louie took up powerlifting. He spent the 1970's training in his basement, his only training partners a power rack, a mirror and an AM radio. (In 1973, Nitro became Louie's training partner: Nitro was a giant pit bull who never missed a single workout, occasionally wore lifting wraps and had a love of donuts).

In 1987 Louie opened his own gym, naming it 'Westside Barbell' in homage to the original California garage gym that had inspired him. And when Nitro passed away, his likeness became the immortal Westside Barbell logo still seen today. Combining many of the ideas from the original Westside with Soviet training approaches (from books Louie read after breaking his back) and Louie's own genius for innovation, the Westside Barbell team would become known as the "Hell's Angels of Powerlifting" for their work with the iron. They would set countless world records, create some of the strongest women who ever lived and invent much of the speciality strength equipment you see in gyms today.

In his 50 year career as a powerlifter, Louie totaled Elite in five different weight classes (the Elite standard is considered to be within the top 1% of competing powerlifters). Even when over the age of 50, Louie achieved a 920 pound squat, a 600 pound bench press and a 722 pound deadlift. In 1991, Louie almost died in surgery and was in the ICU for five days. He was released from the hospital on a Tuesday, and by that Sunday he was bench pressing 350 lbs. despite still having a tracheotomy hole in his throat and stitches from the chest tubes.

He never had a cell phone or social media.

26. Musashi

Miyamoto Musashi was a Japanese swordsman, philosopher, strategist and writer. Known simply as 'Musashi', he fought with a sword in each hand and was undefeated in 61 duels. He was the founder of the Niten Ichiryū and authored both The Book of Five Rings and Dokkōdō (The Path of Aloneness).

Musashi won his first duel at age 13, taking a hostile samurai off his feet with a jiu jitsu throw before swiftly killing him, and in the years that followed he would best many challengers. However his status as a legend would be cemented in his famous duel with Sasaki Kojirō, known as the 'Demon of the Western Provinces'. Kojirō wielded a greatsword so large it was referred to jokingly as a laundry pole and was the master of a two stroke technique called the 'tsubame gaeshi'.

Having agreed to fight each other, a duel was planned on the beaches of the small island of Ganryūjima at the hour of the Dragon (approximately 8am). Despite officials banning spectators, the entire island was quickly filled with onlookers. Kojirō arrived at the appointed time but was then left to wait for hours as Musashi never showed. As he sat around all day enduring the perceived affront to his honor, the heat and the crowds of spectators, Kojirō gradually became more enraged and less focused. Sometime in the mid afternoon, Musashi arrived leisurely in a small fishing boat with no fanfare. Rather than carrying his signature two swords, he carried only a rough wooden sword he had carved from an oar on the ride over, a detail which further enraged his opponent. Musashi approached and began circling with Kojirō, who promptly yelled and leapt forward in his signature attack. Musashi surged forward to meet him and both men's strikes flashed swiftly. The tip of Kojirō's giant blade came so close that it cut off Musashi's headband. The strike of Musashi's wooden blade, on the other hand, landed flush, crushing Kojirō's skull.

Miyamoto Musashi would die at age 62 while holding his sword, having retired to a cave to live as a hermit.

Musashi's 21 Rules of Life:

1. Accept everything just the way it is
2. Do not seek pleasure for its own sake
3. Do not, under any circumstances, depend on a partial feeling
4. Think lightly of yourself and deeply of the world
5. Be detached from desire your whole life long
6. Do not regret what you have done
7. Never be jealous
8. Never let yourself be saddened by a separation
9. Resentment and complaint are appropriate neither for oneself or others
10. Do not let yourself be guided by the feeling of lust or love
11. In all things have no preferences
12. Be indifferent to where you live
13. Do not pursue the taste of good food
14. Do not hold on to possessions you no longer need
15. Do not act following customary beliefs
16. Do not collect weapons or practice with weapons beyond what is useful
17. Do not fear death
18. Do not seek to possess either goods or fiefs for your old age
19. Respect Buddha and the gods without counting on their help
20. You may abandon your own body but you must preserve your honour
21. Never stray from the Way

27. Marvin Hagler

Born in Newark's Central Ward in 1954, "Marvelous" Marvin Hagler was raised by a single mother as one of five children. At age 10 a social worker convinced him to take up boxing and at age 14 he dropped out of school to work in a toy factory to support his siblings and his mother. The Hagler family tenement would be destroyed in the riots of 1967, during which the whole family hid under their mother's bed with bullets passing through the walls above their heads, forcing the family to move to Massachusetts. Though only 14 years old, Marvin claimed to be 16 so he could enter local amateur boxing tournaments (this false birth year would stick with him much of his career).

He would finish his amateur career with a record of 551 yet he struggled to find high profile professional opponents willing to face him. Joe Frazier would tell Hagler, "You have three strikes against you, 'you're black, you're a southpaw, and you're good'." Despite this, he would go on to become one of the best fighters in history, his unparalleled dedication to training and Spartan mindset becoming legend.

While other boxers were partying late and sleeping comfortably in their mansions, Marvin prepared for a prizefight by going into isolation at an abandoned motel on Cape Cod that was described as "a life fit for a Tibetan monk. No family, friends, parties, restaurants, dancing. No sex. No pastries. Lots of situps. Training camps are Spartan by definition. Hagler takes his a step farther. It is more isolated, more desolate, more single minded than most."

Hagler trained 6 days a week, two times per day. Every morning he got up at dawn and ran 6 miles in combat boots (running forwards and backwards), because running shoes were for "softies", and did brutal functional strength workouts, inspired by the old tales of Jack Dempsey cutting down trees with an axe to build power and endurance. His boxing session in the evening was equally intense, sparring and skills training all organized in cycles of 3 minutes of intense work followed by 1 minute of rest.

Hagler's work ethic and training routine made him one of the best middleweight pugilists of all time.

28. Louis Cyr

Said by some to be the strongest man who ever lived, Louis Cyr was born in Quebec, Canada in 1863. Exhibiting an extraordinary degree of strength from an early age, Cyr spent his childhood working winters in a lumber camp and the rest of the year on the family farm. As a young man Cyr liked to demonstrate his strength and after hearing the tale of Milo of Croton (a man who carried a young calf on his shoulders everyday, his strength growing along with the calf, a tale still used today to illustrate the concept of 'progressive overload'), Cyr attempted to do the same. However this plan backfired one day when the calf kicked him in the back and ran away: after that, he switched to quarter mile walks with sacks of grain, adding two pounds each day.

Cyr's career as a strongman began after, at age 17, he single handedly lifted a farmer's wagon out of the mud it was stuck in. His first contest was against Michaud of Quebec, recognized as Canada's strongest man of the time, however Cyr beat him in a stone lifting contest by hoisting a granite boulder weighing 480 lbs. (and less than two years later he was able to shoulder a 514 lbs. stone). Popular with the celebrities and royalty of his day like the Prince of Wales and Queen Victoria, Cyr styled himself as a modern Biblical Samson, a name his mother had called him as a boy, with long locks of hair from which he would frequently hang three 50 lbs. plates. Some of his feats of strength are as follows:

•Lifting eighteen large men on a heavy platform resting across two trestles by ducking beneath the platform, placing his back below the center, and raising both the contraption and the men standing on it clear off the trestles, a weight estimated at 4,000 lbs.

•Resisting the pull of four of Queen Victoria's large draught horses.

Bent Pressing a 273 lbs. dumbbell with one arm (beating Eugene

Sandow's record in the process), as well as pressing a 162 lbs. dumbbell for 36 reps.

•Lifting and carrying one of the Dinnie Stones.

•Deadlifting 525 lbs. on a thick bar with one arm.

•Performing a crucifix hold with 97 lbs. in his right hand and 88 lbs. in his left.

•Performed a stunt of stacking four fifty pound weights on top of his flexed arm and balancing them while walking across the room.

•Cyr participated in a wrestling match with a giant. Both men weighed in at 365 lbs., however Cyr was measured at a height of 5'8" while his opponent was measured at 8'2" inches. Cyr won the match.

29. George De Relwyskow

George de Relwyskow was born in Kensington, England in 1887 to Russian immigrants. Initially taking an interest in wrestling as a way to stay in shape while studying as an artist, he quickly became a dominant force in British wrestling. By 1908 he had won thirty five open competitions as well as the English amateur championships back to back in 1907 and 1908, at both lightweight and middleweight. This culminated in his competition in the 1908 London Olympic Games in Freestyle Wrestling where he competed at both lightweight and middleweight, winning a gold medal at lightweight and a silver medal at middleweight. He was the youngest winner of an Olympic gold medal for wrestling (a record that would stand until 1976).

When World War 1 broke out, de Relwyskow was on a wrestling tour of South America. Hearing of the hostilities, he returned to England and enlisted in the British Army. Serving with the Australian Infantry, he instructed men in bayonet fighting, gymnastics and unarmed combat. In 1918 he would create the 'Army System of Wrestling', which was taught to Allied forces to prepare them for the gritty combat of World War 1. His system spread like wildfire, proving highly effective in the close quarters fighting seen in trench warfare where men often battled face to face with hands, brass knuckles, knives and shovels.

After the war, George would serve as a trainer for the British team in the 1924 Olympic Games in Paris. However at the outbreak of World War 2, he enlisted her again. This time he would serve as an instructor in Unarmed Combat and Silent Killing with the Special Operations Executive (SOE), teaching soldiers not only in Britain but also in Canada at the Special Training School 103 (known as "Camp X"), before being deployed to Burma. It was during this time that he trained and instructed under the legendary William E. Fairbairn, who adopted and taught many of his wrestling techniques.

Relwyskow died at his Leeds home in 1942, his wife Clara at his side.

30. Herschel Walker

One of six siblings born on a small farm in rural Georgia, Herschel Walker would go on to be one of the best athletes in NFL history. He also thrived in collegiate track and field, earned a 5th degree black belt in taekwondo, competed as an Olympic bobsledder and later even fought in mixed martial arts (in his 40's).

However he did not always show such athletic aptitude. As a boy he was short, chubby and uncoordinated, as well as affected by a speech impediment. As a result, he was frequently bullied. This continued until sixth grade when Herschel approached a local track and field coach for help getting "bigger, stronger, faster and better at sports". The coach told him this task wouldn't be easy, however it would be simple:

Do push ups, sit ups and sprints.

You can't make excuses in life, you've got to get it done, his parents had always told him.

So he did.

"There weren't any weights then at school, of course, and we sure didn't have any out in the country, but I used what I had, and that was the living room floor and the dirt road that ran from the highway out front up the hill to our house. I did my pushups and my situps on the floor most of the time, and I did all my sprints up that hill out front," he said.

Herschel worked tirelessly and before long he expanded on the coach's instructions, adding in chin ups and squats to a daily body weight routine that had grown to 2,0003,000 total reps (a routine he continued into his 50's). Soon after, he also began doing weighted carries using bales of hay, trying to keep up with the family horse on runs and training in martial arts. By then he was excelling in multiple sports and had become the valedictorian and president of the honor society at his high school.

Despite focusing heavily on calisthenics, Walker built the strength necessary to bench press 375 pounds in college, setting the record at the University of Georgia (where he was an AllAmerican in both football and track).

31. Rena Kanokogi

Rena Kanokogi was a renowned JewishAmerican judo expert who, disguised as a man, won a YMCA judo tournament in 1959.

Born in Brooklyn in 1935 and raised in Coney Island, her early life was not a stable one. She began working at age 7 and later, in her adolescence, would lead a youth street gang known as the Apaches. In her teens she began lifting her brother's weights and working out on the punching bag at the local gymnasium. Eventually a male friend would show Rena a judo technique that he had learned, immediately capturing her interest, later recalling that she was attracted to the art because it calmed her down and helped her develop self control. Rena began training fanatically in her local neighborhood, her grit and tenacity earning her the nickname 'Rusty' (named after a tough local street dog). However despite numerous attempts, she was banned from participating in competitions due to her gender.

Rena sidestepped the obstacle of gender altogether by entering the 1959 YMCA Judo Championship in Utica, New York, disguised as a man. Technically she was not breaking any rules, as women were not explicitly barred from the competition (no woman had ever tried to participate before so there wasn't even a place on the tournament application to indicate gender). Having cut her hair short and taped down her breasts, she was originally slated to serve her team as an alternate before a teammate was injured and she was called upon to compete. Rena won her match, and her team won the championship. However, afterwards the tournament organizer pulled her aside and asked if she was a woman. She confirmed that she was and was promptly stripped of her medal.

In 1962, Rena traveled to Tokyo, Japan where she was admitted into the Kodokan Judo Institute. After allegedly "pulverizing" all of the students in the female group, she became the first woman ever allowed to train in the men's group at the Kodokan. At the Kodokan she would go on to be promoted to the rank of 2nd dan and would meet her future husband, Ryohei Kanokogi, a judoka from the Nichidai University judo team.

The couple would marry in New York in 1964.

32. Kazushi 'The Gracie Killer' Sakuraba

Born in 1969, Kazushi Sakuraba fell in love with grappling as a boy after reading a Japanese graphic novel called Tiger Mask. He began wrestling at age 15, eventually achieving the rank of second in the nation in high school. On the freestyle wrestling team at Chuo University, a team who's past products included Olympic gold medalists Shozo Sasahara and Osamu Watanabe, he would serve as team captain and see much success, including victory over future Olympic bronze medalist Takuya Ota.

After college, Sakuraba worked as a pro wrestler while training catch wrestling under the great Billy Robison. This all changed when the UFC came to Japan. Although not invited initially, Sakuraba filled in at the last minute for an injured colleague. As a pro wrestler, he was not taken seriously. Additionally, he smoked cigarettes, drank a lot and didn't take steroids. As if that wasn't enough, the UFC Japan event was a heavyweight tournament and Sakuraba only weighed 182 lbs. (after bulking up from his 150 lbs. natural weight). Having falsely reported himself as weighing 203 lbs. in order to gain entry, he ended up fighting in the championship against 240 lbs. Brazilian Jiujitsu black belt and mixed martial arts champion Marcus Silveira.

To most the idea of a 182 lbs pro wrestler, fighting a 240 lbs BJJ black belt and mixed martial arts champ is unimaginable, and for good reason, but Sakuraba was known to be undeterred by such things. The match opened and before long the giant Brazilian managed to take Sakuraba's back, putting him in a highly dangerous position. Sakuraba managed to escape the position but ended up in Silveira's guard, and soon found his arm trapped in the much larger man's kimura. The situation looked grim until Sakuraba, his arm still trapped, passed the guard and scrambled around to reverse his opponent's kimura into an armbar of his own.

Silveira tapped.

Sakuraba would become one of the greatest martial artists of all time, beating the champions of 13 different MMA organizations (many of whom were several weight classes above him). He even became known as 'The Gracie Killer' with wins over four members of the legendary Gracie family: Royler Gracie, Renzo Gracie, Ryan Gracie and Royce Gracie.

33. Martin 'Farmer' Burns

Martin Burns was born in a log cabin on a farm in Cedar County, Iowa. Growing up amidst the Civil War, he was surrounded from an early age by the sport of wrestling, a common activity among enlisted soldiers at a time when wrestling was gaining popularity and even the President was a wrestler.

At age 11 his father died, leaving him to support a mother, brother and five sisters. Burns worked at a nearby farm for $12 per month to support them and it was this labor that enabled Burns to develop his remarkable physical strength (he was later said to have a 20" neck and be able to survive a hanging simply by flexing it), even competing in strongman competitions. All the while, Burns continued to meticulously develop his skill in catch wrestling (a no holds barred grappling style of pins and submissions). By combining his physical conditioning, meticulous skills training and his intellectual approach to the sport itself, Burns became dominant. Making waves, the man now known as "Farmer" Burns became known for dangerous maneuvers such as the hammerlock, double wrist lock, chicken wing and a variety of toe holds.

On May 13, 1891, Burns scored his biggest win yet when he pinned renowned Japanese wrestler and former challenger to the great William Muldoon, Sorakichi Matsuda, in just four minutes. In his next bout, Burns proved himself to be the world's best all around grappler when he defeated Evan "Strangler" Lewis, the American GrecoRoman Wrestling Champion as well as the CatchAsCatchCan Champion, by pin.

After retirement, Burns opened a school in Omaha and coached legends such as Frank Gotch, Ralph Parcaut and Joseph "Toots" Mondt. He would also write 'The Lessons in Wrestling and Physical Culture', described as the "wrestlers bible", which incorporated breathing techniques, calisthenics and Eastern martial arts principles.

Famed for his strength training, Farmer Burns had an infamous workout routine consisting of:

Phase 1: Warm up, stretching movement.
Phase 2: High intensity/heavy dumbbell routine.
Phase 3: Intense exercise utilizing the weight of a partner's body.

34. Willie Pep

Guglielmo Papaleo, better known as 'Willie Pep', was an American professional boxer and two time World Featherweight champion between the years of 1942 and 1950. An inspiration to Muhammad Ali, Pep was one of the fastest, slickest and most elusive boxers ever to set foot in the ring. Sugar Ray Robinson described fighting Pep as "battling a man in a hall of mirrors" and after Willy won his 199th fight, opponent Kid Campeche described his experience fighting Pep by saying, "fighting Willie Pep is like trying to stomp out a grass fire." It was even said that he is the only fighter to ever win a round without throwing a punch.

In 1937, Pep was a fifteen year old shoeshine boy in downtown Hartford, Connecticut when he started boxing in the amateurs. His father only made $15 per week so when Pep realized he could make more from one fight than in a week of shining shoes, he turned his focus to boxing. In 1940 he went pro and by 1942 he was the Featherweight champion of the world. Pep would spend the next several years on a dominant run as champion, defending his belt repeatedly with all the style and finesse he had come to be known for. However on January 5, 1947, the plane Pep was riding in crashed and he suffered catastrophic, near fatal injuries. Amazingly, he returned to the ring just five months later. Despite the accident in January and months of recovery, Pep would go on to fight ten times in the remainder of 1947. He finished the year with a record of 10-0.

In his 26 year career, Pep boxed a total of 1,956 rounds in the 241 bouts. His final record was 229–11–1 with 65 knockouts. In the fights following his plane crash and rehabilitation, Pep would go 121-10-1 (including a record of 9-1 after he launched a comeback in 1965 at age 42).

Pep was inducted into the International Boxing Hall of Fame in 1990 and was voted as the #1 featherweight of the century by the Associated Press and the #1 featherweight of all time by the International Boxing Research Organization in 2005.

35. Aaron Molyneaux Hewlett

America's first ever Superintendent of Physical Education in higher education and the first black instructor at Harvard University, physical culturist and functional strength pioneer Aaron Molyneaux Hewlett, was born in 1820. A native of Brooklyn, he spent his early years wrestling and boxing and was described by The New York Clipper, the leading New York sports newspaper of the day, as "one of the best boxers in Brooklyn".

In 1854 he quit his job as a porter and opened a sparring academy at his home, known as "Molyneaux House". In addition to the conventional strength and conditioning methods of the day, Hewlett trained his fighters using many of the functional methods witnessing a revival today, particularly the use of the weighted club and the medicine ball. In fact, it is a picture of Hewlett that is the first known photo of a medicine ball in American history. The picture also included a wide variety of training equipment: large wooden clubs similar to the joris used by Indian wrestlers, Indian club/dumbbell hybrids, medicine balls, boxing gloves, large globe dumbbells and an exercise wand.

In 1859 Hewlett moved to Cambridge, Massachusetts and became the first black teacher at Harvard University, earning the position of superintendent of the Harvard Gymnasium for over a decade, teaching gymnastics, boxing, and wrestling. After Hewlett had been working at Harvard for a decade, a local Boston paper stated that Harvard's "Athletics have come almost to rank with Mathematics". In addition, Hewlett operated his own training hall, the Cambridge Gymnasium, with his wife Virginia, a prominent gymnast in her own right. This impressive facility catered to men, women, and children.

Hewlett was also a passionate civil rights activist. His daughter, Virginia Hewlett Douglass, married the son of abolitionist Frederick Douglass, and became a prominent suffragist. His son, Emanuel D. Molyneaux Hewlett, was the first Black man to graduate from the Boston University School of Law and was also very active in the civil rights movement.

Aaron Molyneaux Hewlett died in 1871 when he unexpectedly succumbed to an infection from an abscess on his head.

36. Crazy Horse

Crazy Horse was born as Čháŋ Óhaŋ (Among the Trees), most likely between 1840 and 1842. His parents belonged to different bands of the Lakota Sioux, his father belonging to the Oglala and his mother belonging to the Miniconjou. When he was four years old, his mother hung herself from a tree.

When he was a boy, his camp was entered by Lt. John Lawrence Gratton and 29 U.S. troopers, intent on arresting a Sioux man for 'stealing' a cow that had wandered into camp. When the soldiers fatally shot Chief Conquering Bear, the Lakota promptly killed all 30 soldiers.

After witnessing the event Crazy Horse began to have visions.

"He went out on a vision quest to seek guidance without going through the traditional procedures first. In his vision, a warrior on his horse rode out of a lake and the horse seemed to float and dance throughout the vision. He wore simple clothing, no face paint, his hair down with just a feather in it, and a small brown stone behind his ear. Bullets and arrows flew around him as he charged forward, but neither he nor his horse was hit. A thunderstorm came over the warrior, and his people grabbed hold of his arms trying to hold him back. The warrior broke their hold and then lightning struck him, leaving a lightning symbol on his cheek, and white marks like hailstones appeared on his body... As the vision ended, he heard a red tailed hawk shrieking off in the distance."

Adopting a lightning symbol on his cheek and hailstones on his body as war paint, Crazy Horse accepted his destiny. This culminated on June 25, 1876 when George Armstrong Custer led the 7th Cavalry in an attack on a large encampment of Cheyenne and Lakota bands along the Little Bighorn River, killing noncombatants and warriors alike. Looking down at the masses of US Cavalry, he reportedly said only, "today is a good day to die" before charging forward on his faithful horse, Stone.

Crazy Horse and his men would shock the world when they shattered the 7th Cavalry and killed Custer himself in the Battle of Little Bighorn in the US's biggest defeat of the Indian Wars.

37. Mike Tyson

In his prime, Mike Tyson's entire life revolved around being the baddest man alive. His daily routine was virtually identical from one day to the next and consisted of 2,000 squats, 500 dips, 500 pushups, 500 neck bridges, 1,000 situps and 500 weighted shrugs. He ate the same meals every day, down to his daily snack of a protein shake with bananas and his favorite dessert: Cap'N Crunch cereal.

His day was structured as follows:

•Early morning – wake up at 4AM and run 35 miles followed by pushups, situps and squats.

•Breakfast: oatmeal, milk and multivitamin. Followed by a nap.

•Noon: Sit Ups, dips, pushups, shrugs, and neck bridges. Followed by sparring on contact days.

•Lunch: chicken, rice and orange juice.

•Midafternoon: Punching bag, slip bag, focus mitts, speed bag and Cus D'Amato's famous Willie bag. Followed by jumping rope, more pushups, situps and squats and 60 minutes on a workout bike.

•Snack: protein shake with multiple bananas.

•Early evening: Dips, shrugs, neck bridges and shadow boxing (focusing on one technique at a time).

•Dinner: steak and pasta. Cap'N Crunch Cereal for dessert.

•After dinner: 30 minutes on an exercise bike.

•Late evening: Film study.

(He trained six days per week and rested on Sunday).

In prison, Mike worked out relentlessly. The following is an old prison squat workout favored by Mike Tyson to help condition his legs when he was locked up.

Complete it as many times as necessary:
• Line up ten cards facedown in a straight line on the ground with 4" between each.
• Begin by standing over the first card and squatting down to pick it up.
• Holding the first card, take a step forward to the second card. Squat down and place the card you just picked up on top of the second card. (At this point, you'll have no cards in your hand, and 2 cards will be one on top of the other on the ground below you).
• Squat once and pick up the first card.
• Squat once and pick up the second card.
• Take a step forward to the third card, squat down, and place one of the two cards in your hand on top of the card on the ground.
• Now squat down and place the other card on top of the cards on the ground.
• Squat one time each to pick up the three cards one by one.
• Take a step forward to the fourth card, and repeat this process until you've made it through all ten cards.

38. Edward Payton Weston

Long distance endurance events have always captured the imagination, and people have been running ultramarathons since before recorded history. However the dawn of ultra endurance events in the modern age began in the late 18th and 19th centuries. Ultramarathoners, known then as 'pedestrians', left crowds in awe with their seemingly superhuman stamina and unbreakable willpower, and events began to draw large crowds. By the mid19th century races were being held in indoor stadiums full of finely dressed spectators that included the aristocracy, not unlike fancy horse shows of the day. However as refined as the presentation and spectators could be, the track below was a gritty world and it was not uncommon for athletes to utilize nitroglycerin, cocaine or opium in an attempt to dull the pain or keep them awake during races.

As with most sports, nationalistic loyalties developed within the sport. Pedestrianism had been invented in England and the British considered their ultramarathoners the best in the world, on a level all their own. However soon the Brits began hearing reports of pedestrians in America covering vast distances, distances of hundreds of miles that didn't even seem possible. These reports were met with skepticism, disdain or outright accusations of dishonesty, with a leading British sportswriter saying, "Not to mince matters, the reason we Englishmen only believe what we see of American prowess, is the extreme untruthfulness of American sportsmen."

A series of challenges was issued back and forth across the Atlantic, culminating in the first ultramarathon battle between Britain and America. The British would be represented by William T. Perkins, England's best pedestrian, described as being 5' 6", 132 pounds, with broad shoulders and had very muscular thighs. American would be represented by Edward Payson Weston, a man who had years prior walked the 478 miles from Boston to Washington DC to attend Abraham Lincoln's inauguration after losing a bet with a friend (he arrived at 5pm the day of the inauguration and still had the strength to attend the event that evening). The competition would put the two men together to see who could cover the most distance in 24 hours, an at 9:25 p.m. on February 8, 1876, the duel started in London in front of 5,000 spectators. The British were relieved to see Perkins take an early lead, a lead that seemed to build steadily. However at the 50 mile mark, Perkins started to slow and sensing weakness, Weston began to increase his pressure. At mile 59 Weston finally passed the Brit, who's socks and shoes were so soaked in blood they had to be cut off his feet.

In the end Weston finished 109 miles in the allotted 24 hours, while Perkins was forced to tap out after 65 miles.

39. William E. Fairbairn

William E. Fairbairn was a British police officer in Shanghai, Royal Marine and close quarters combat instructor to commandos. Fairbairn served with the Royal Marine Light Infantry before joining the Shanghai Municipal Police in 1907. Assigned to one of the city's red light districts, Fairbairn participated in hundreds of street fights throughout his 20 year career. His body, arms, legs and the palms of his hands were covered with knife scars. He later organized and led the city's riot squad as well as designing equipment for the department, including a metal lined bulletproof vest designed to stop a high velocity Mauser pistol round.

At the outbreak of World War 2, Fairbairn was recruited by the British Special Operations Executive. He would go on to train British, American, Canadian and Dutch special forces in hand to hand combat, pistol shooting and knife fighting. He would also help make instructional films on close quarters combat for agents of the U.S. Office of Strategic Services (the precursor to the Central Intelligence Agency). Fairbairn believed that any idea of gentlemanly conduct or fighting fair should be abandoned in combat: "Get tough, get down in the gutter, win at all costs... I teach what is called 'Gutter Fighting.' There's no fair play, no rules except one: kill or be killed". To this end he utilized his expertise in boxing, wrestling, jujutsu, judo and savate to design his own martial art, known as 'Defendu', which consisted of a savage mix of jujutsu, boxing and street fighting.

He also designed the famous Fairbairn Sykes Fighting knife, a stiletto style fighting knife used by British Special Forces, as well as the Smatchet, a combination of a machete and a bolo. William Fairbairn died in 1960 but his influence and contributions are still felt in the special operations community today.

He was even said to be the inspiration for the James Bond character 'Q'.

40. Kimura

Born on September 10, 1917, Masahiko Kimura(木村 政彦) is widely considered one of the greatest judoka of all time, as well as the strongest man in the history of the sport of judo. The reverse ude garami arm lock is now called the "Kimura" in his honor, as a result of his famous victory over Brazilian Jiu Jitsu pioneer Hélio Gracie, which is still a common technique utilized in BJJ, mixed martial arts and hand to hand combat.

Kimura began training judo at age 9. At age 18 he became the youngest ever 5th degree black belt after defeating eight opponents in a row at the Kodokan Judo Institute. He reportedly lost only four matches in his lifetime, all in 1935.
After these losses he considered quitting judo, but instead decided to rededicate himself and took his training to another level altogether. He increased his strength and conditioning, practiced his signature osoto gari throw against a tree and participated in sparring sessions at Tokyo Police and Kodokan dojos so intense that numerous opponents were knocked unconscious by his throws.

He would never lose another match.

Legendary Karate Master Mas Oyama admitted that Kimura was the only man he had ever seen who trained harder than he did, and Kimura's peak daily routine, which allegedly took about 9 hours to finish and was completed 6 days per week, was as follows:

•1,000 Push Ups.
•Bunny Hop 1 kilometer.
•Headstand 3 × 3 Minutes.
•Judo Throws 100 Reps.
•One Arm Barbell Press: 15 Reps each side or Bench Press: 3 Sets: 3, 2, and 1 Reps.
•200 Situps off Partner's Back.
•200 Squats with Partner, Log, Barbell or Sandbag.
•Submission Drills 100 Reps.
•500 Hand Strikes.
•Judo Entries 100 Reps.
•Judo Randori "X" × 3 Minute Rounds.
•Practice Throws Against a Tree 1 Hour.
•Additional Judo Practice 1 Hour.

41. John Wesley Southard

On June 14, 1927, eleven Native American men lined up in front of City Hall in San Francisco for the Indian Redwood Marathon, a 480 mile race up the coast through mountains, rivers and redwood forests to Grants Pass, Oregon. The race itself proved to present difficulties for the runners beyond simple distance. Despite frequently changing shoes, the runners quickly ran their feet raw on the road and soon developed respiratory issues from constantly breathing the exhaust and brake dust from the automobiles of media, spectators and race organizers that crowded the roads around them.

One participant was named John Wesley 'Mad Bull' Southard, a man of mixed white and Karuk heritage and the oldest male of 12 children. John grew up as a hunter, living his life believing it was a disgrace to buy meat since the mountains he lived in were full of deer, and it was trekking through the mountains chasing deer that introduced him to long distance running. As a boy, he was known to frequently run around his charter school each morning to build up his weak body. He believed in maintaining good health and always abstained from using tobacco or alcohol. Him and the other runners of the Karuk tribe had a strict daily regimen starting with a 5am swim in the cold river followed by a light run before breakfast. They would then spend the day running and hiking over mountain trails, often running the 60 miles up the Klamath River to Hamburg and back.

Throughout the race Southard would get only one night of sleep, subsisting primarily on 1 hour naps and a mix of raw eggs and orange juice. He had a strategy of power hiking the steep hills while running the slopes and flats, a strategy still used by top ultramarathon runners today.
In the end he crossed the finish line at 12:16am on the eighth day of the race, winning with a time of seven days, twelve hours and thirty four minutes to claim the first prize of $1,000.

42. Steve Mcqueen

Steve McQueen, known as the King of Cool, came from humble roots. Dyslexic and partially deaf, he spent his childhood fleeing the abuse of a string of stepfathers and committing crimes with street gangs, eventually landing him in a juvenile correctional home. After a short stint working at a brothel in the Dominican Republic, McQueen joined the U.S. Marine Corps where he saved the lives of five men by pulling them from a tank before it fell through the ice in an Arctic training maneuver. McQueen would later describe his time in the Marines as the formative time of his life, saying "they made a man out of me."

Throughout his life, McQueen maintained a disciplined workout schedule. In his early days this consisted of hard rounds at a local boxing gym and barbell lifts using an old metal street sign. As he became more successful, his equipment and training evolved. However through it all, he maintained a highly balanced training protocol. Unusual in his day, McQueen lifted weights for two hours every day along with long rucks or five mile runs every morning, even though he was a heavy smoker. As much as his boxing, lifting and running, he was known for his martial arts training with Bruce Lee. The two became great friends and McQueen would act as a pallbearer at Bruce's funeral. He would also go on to train with Chuck Norris and Pat E. Johnson.

McQueen would maintain this disciplined routine until he was rendered incapable by the cancer that eventually killed him in 1980.

43. Donald Dinnie

Donald Dinnie was possibly the best all around athlete in history. A Highland strongman, wrestler and track athlete, his mix of functional strength, endurance and athleticism is all but unheard of, before or since. Winning the Scottish Highland Games 21 years in a row, Dinnie could also run the 100 yard dash in 10.4 seconds. Far more than simply a strongman, according to the British Broadcasting Corporation Dinnie's documented achievements consist of winning over 2,000 hammer throwing contests, over 2,000 wrestling matches, 200 weightlifting contests and about 500 running and hurdle events.

His most famous feat was his lifting of a pair of large stones located in Potarch, Aberdeenshire, Scotland. He reportedly not only lifted but carried the stones barehanded across the width of the Potarch Bridge, a distance of 17 feet and 1.5 inches in 1860, after which they were named the 'Dinnie Stanes' in his honor. The stones themselves are composed of solid granite and have attached iron rings. They have a combined weight of 733 lbs., with the larger stone weighing 414 lb and the smaller stone weighing 318 lbs.). They are so heavy that they were reportedly selected as counterweights for the Potarch Bridge in the 1830's.

Over the course of an athletic career spanning more than 50 years he would be the victor of over 11,000 athletic events. At 6'1" and 210 lbs. his track and field numbers were officially recorded as:

•High jump – 6 feet 1 inch (1.85 m).

•Long jump – 20 feet 1 inch (6.12 m).

•100 yards (91 m) run – 10.4 sec.

•Hammer throw, fair stand – 104 feet 6 inches (31.85 m) (1871).

•Shot put (16 pounds/7.3 kg) stone – 49 feet 6 inches (15.09 m) (1868).

•Throw 22 pounds (10.0 kg) weight by the ring, fair stand – 39 feet 9 inches (12.12 m) (1868).

•Throw 56 pounds (25 kg) weight by the ring, fair stand – 29 feet 4 inches (8.94 m) (1868).

•Victor of over 2,000 hammer throwing contests, over 2,000 wrestling matches, 200 weightlifting contests, and about 500 running and hurdle events.

44. Horatius

In 509 BC, the Etruscan King Lars Porsena marched on Rome at the head of a large army. Concentrating his forces on the Etruscan side of the Tiber, proceeded towards the Pons Sublicius, the only local bridge across the river that was separating the invading army from Rome. The Romans waited in the Naevian Meadow, blocking their way. Battle ensued and the Etruscan right wing succeeded in breaking through, wounding two Roman commanders and causing the Roman line to collapse. As the army of Rome retreated back over the bridge, three men stood their ground: commanders Spurius Lartius and Titus Herminius Aquilinus, plus Publius Horatius Cocles, a junior officer who had been on guard at the bridge.

Dionysius explains, "Herminius and Lartius, their defensive arms being now rendered useless by the continual blows they received, began to retreat gradually. They ordered Horatius to retreat with them, but he stood his ground. Understanding the threat to Rome if the enemy were to cross the river, he ordered his men to destroy the bridge. The enemy was shocked not only by Horatius' suicidal last stand, but also by his decision to use a pile of bodies as a shield wall. Horatius was struck by enemy missiles many times including a spear in the buttocks. Hearing word from his men they'd torn up the bridge, he leaped fully armed into the river and swam across, emerging on the shore
without having lost any of his weapons. For his service, Horatius was awarded with as much of the public land as he himself could plow in one day".

XXVI
But the Consul's brow was sad,
And the Consul's speech was low,
And darkly looked he at the wall, And darkly at the foe.
"Their van will be upon us
Before the bridge goes down;
And if they once may win the bridge, What hope to save the town?"

XXVII
Then out spake brave Horatius, The Captain of the Gate:
"To every man upon this earth
Death cometh soon or late.
And how can man die better
Than facing fearful odds,
For the ashes of his fathers,

And the temples of his gods"

45. Gustaf Håkansson

The Sverigeloppet is a 1,096 mile bike race across the country of Sweden. Due to his advanced age, Gustaf Håkansson's application to the race was denied. In addition to being 66 years old, he also had a long white beard that was the result of a promise to never cut it following an argument with his barber. Here Gustaf's stubbornness again revealed itself. Refusing to take 'No' for an answer, Gustaf crossed the starting line one minute after the last of the competitors had taken off, wearing a shirt on which he had written the number '0' instead of a regulation racing jersey.

Despite being older than the rest of the competitors, he slowly but surely started to pass them by. The younger athletes may have been faster but when they stopped to sleep every night, Gustaf kept pedaling. After 6 days, 14 hours and 20 minutes, he arrived at the finish line (more than 24 hours ahead of the second place finisher). A national hero, he was called 'The Steel Grandpa' and was given an audience with the King of Sweden the very next day.

However Gustaf was not done just yet. Eight years later, at 74 years of age, he would ride his bike more than 3,000 miles from Sweden to Jerusalem in order to tour the city's holy sites. He would continue his biking journeys until after his 100th birthday.

He died from natural causes at 101 years old.

MISCELLANEA

46. The Belt System In Martial Arts

One of the most recognizable aspects of modern martial arts is the use of colored belts to rank the skill level or chart the progression of practitioners, starting at white belt and ending at black belt (or red belt). Even outside of martial arts, referring to someone as a black belt in their craft signifies a high level of skill or accomplishment. The belt system itself was said to originate in Japan: the legend states that martial arts students all began wearing white belts ('obi') before years of dirt, blood and sweat turned them black.

What is known for sure is as far back as the 9th century, certificates known as Menkyo (免許) were used to demonstrate rank. However in 1883, judo founder Kanō Jigorō implemented a two belt ranking system (white and black) in order to better match competitors with those of comparable skill level. In the following decades the belt system would be adopted by karate instructors before eventually becoming universal. The full system of colored belts we see today was devised by judo master Kawaishi Mikonosuke while he was in Paris teaching jujutsu to the French Police in the 1930's.

The first official belt ranking system for Brazilian Jiu-jitsu was created in 1967. Prior to this there were only three belt colors: the white belt was for students, the light blue belt for instructors and the dark blue for masters. (Note: this is why, despite being a 7th degree black belt, Royce Gracie still wears a dark blue belt as an homage to his father and early history of Brazilian Jiu-jitsu).

47. How Old Is The Kettlebell?

Kettlebells were not invented in 18th century Russia and they were not brought to America by Pavel Tatsouline. Kettlebells have existed in many forms throughout many cultures going back thousands of years: tribes of the Scottish Highlands fixed iron handles to stones, soldiers and martial artists in ancient China trained using stone locks and the ancient Greeks carved 'halteres' of solid stone. The kettlebell, along with the weighted club or mace, is one of the oldest and most consistent functional strength tools in human history, with intricately carved kettlebells being recovered from as far back as the 3rd millennium BC.

48. The Training And Diet Of 19Th Century Boxers

A description of training for British boxers in the 18th and 19th centuries, from 'Boxiana' by Pierce Egan (the man who created the term 'The Sweet Science' to describe boxing), published in 1813:

"The skilled trainer attends to the state of the bowels, of the lungs, and the skin; and uses such means as will reduce the fat, at the same time, invigorate the muscular fibres (sic)...he is sweated by walking under a load of clothes, and by lying between feather-beds. His limbs are roughly rubbed. his diet is beef or mutton: his drink strong ale...(He) enters upon his training with a regular course of physic, which consists of three doses...he must rise at five in the morning, run half a mile at top speed uphill and walk six miles at a moderate pace, coming in about seven to breakfast, which should be beef-steaks or mutton chops with stale bread and old beer. After breakfast he must again walk six miles at a moderate pace, at at twelve lie down in bed without his close half an hour...on getting up, he must walk four miles and return by four to dinner...Immediately after dinner he must resume his exercise by running half a mile at top speed, and walking six miles at moderate pace."

49. Jack Dempsey's Training Tips For Fighters

I. Sparring

"Although some exercises help condition and others speed improvement, there's one all-important activity that assists both. That activity is sparring. THERE IS NO SUBSTITUTE FOR SPARRING. You must spar regularly and often..."

II. Heavy bag

"Work on the bags will develop all the muscles you use in punching, and it will give "tone" to them. Your chest, shoulders and arms will take on that sleek, well-rounded appearance that distinguishes the bodies of most fighters from those of ordinary chaps."

III. Shadowboxing

"Shadow-boxing is the next best exercise for the twofold purpose of conditioning and sharpening. It might be described as fighting an imaginary opponent. It is particularly helpful in developing footwork."

V. Jumping Rope

"In skipping, you do not jump with both feet at the same time; nor do you skip with a hippity-hop, like a school girl. Instead, you bounce off one foot and then off the other."

IV. Running

"After you've become accustomed to roadwork and your feet have hardened, mix up your runs by sprinting for 100 yards, then jogging, then shadow-boxing for a few seconds, then jogging, then sprinting, etc."

VI. Calisthenics

Dempsey favored a wide range of calisthenics for strength and conditioning, but paid particular attention to push ups and core work.

VII. Accessories
Dempsey recommends using additional accessories to build the neck, core and hands. Pulleys, harnesses, grip training, medicine balls and chopping wood all played a part.

50. The Longest Boxing Match In History

The longest boxing match in recorded history took place in New Orleans, Louisiana on April 6, 1893, between lightweights Andy Bowen and Jack Burke. Bowen had originally been scheduled to fight another opponent, however when the man dropped out of the fight, his trainer, Jack Burke, stepped up in his place. This change would lead to one of the most brutal bouts of pugilism of all time.

The fight took place at the Olympics Club, where Jim Corbett would make history two years later by defeating John L Sullivan for the world heavyweight title. It would devolve into a brutal slugfest that lasted 110 rounds, over seven hours and 19 minutes in length. At round 108, with no clear end in sight, referee John Duffy made the decision that if no winner had emerged in the next 2 rounds, the bout would be ruled a "no contest". With both men having become too dazed and tired to come out of their corners after 110 rounds, Duffy indeed declared the match a no contest.

Both men were battered beyond recognition. Burke broke all the bones in both of his hands and was bedridden for six weeks. Bowen would die in the ring the next year, failing to wake up after a knock out, likely due to damage sustained in his match with Burke.

51. The Diets Of Ancient Athletes

Ancient athletes, like those of today, sought to find the best diets to improve their performance. They consulted physicians, athletic trainers and past traditions alike, resulting in extensive studies, debates and trends among and within cultures. And when a highly successful champion emerged, many would seek to emulate or reproduce their diet and training regiment. For instance, one year the Ancient Olympics was won by a man who said he only ate meat resulting in athletes all over Greece going carnivore (the same thing happened another year when a different champion swore that massive quantities of honey were the secret to his success). The question of diet may not have been complicated by modern marketing trends however people were no less serious in their approach to the foods they believed increased human performance. Food selection, animal husbandry, fertilizer, soil, individual plant selection, curing and packaging all played a part, and could vary widely even among athletes within the same population or culture.

In Ancient Greece it was common for athletes of all types to eat dried fruit, cheese and ancient grains, but it was believed the best type of meat varied depending on the athlete's sport. For wrestlers, it was believed the best meat was either wild boar or that of a rooster who had survived a cockfight. Strength athletes preferred beef while Olympic jumpers and runners preferred goat and deer respectively. Spartans, perennial top performers in both sport and warfare, ate primarily game meat.

In Ancient Rome, it was believed that the 'Strong Foods' were grain, domesticated red meat, game meat, large birds (goose and peacock, for example), honey and cheese. However Galen, the legendary researcher and physician, was adamant that pork and beans should form the basis of an athlete's diet based on his years working with gladiators. While in Ancient India, which was largely vegetarian, grapplers sought calories from milk, almonds, ghee and dried fruit, while avoiding spicy or sour foods.

While the details vary, one thing that cannot be denied is that even the ancients observed the obvious correlation between high protein, high micronutrient diets and improved athletic performance.

52. The Dub Method

The Dub Method is a training method commonly utilized by inmates in the prisons and jails houses of the United States. If one was to peek into the solitary confinement cells of Pelican Bay or watch the workout yard at San Quentin, they would see some of the fittest inmates present utilizing the Dub Method. The method is a high volume bodyweight approach, elegant in both its simplicity and brutality. Contrary to popular belief, there are no weights available to prisoners in the US Correctional System. As such, inmate workouts require more functionality, creativity and volume than your average day in the gym. When considering all of the potential applications, movements and variations, it is easy to see that possibilities are vast. However the method itself is very simple and can be summed up in one sentence:

"20 sets of 20".

For example, on a push day a prisoner would simply do 20 sets of 20 push ups. Once that inmate is able to complete their twenty sets, they would switch to Hindu push ups or push ups with their feet elevated to add difficulty, before eventually adding another block. They would then do the same with their squats, burpees, sit ups, dips, rows, curls (using garbage bags filled with water) and shadow boxing combos. This high volume approach isn't just a prison anecdote, it improves strength, endurance, coordination and fortitude across the board while also defying stereotypes about calisthenics by packing on quality muscle.

Personal note:
My interest in strength training was born while I was serving time as a young man, and I learned the Dub Method from a gang member who was an inmate on my cell block. At the time I had been staying in the same cell where they would later put the Golden State Killer, a monstrous serial murderer who had killed dozens of innocent people over decades, before overpopulation saw me transferred. Upon arrival on the new yard I noticed a muscular Crip who stood around 6'4" was easily 250 lbs. doing what seemed like an impossible amount of dips all alone.

Eventually I asked him a thing or two about training. We couldn't workout together as we belonged to different races, but we would train in adjacent areas and talk casually as I picked his brain. He was a firm believer in daily calisthenics and during his years of imprisonment he had utilized the Dub Method, and his admittedly insane genetics, to build both a body like an NFL linebacker and a level of functional strength and movement I've frankly never seen before or since in someone that size. Learning from him, I utilized the Dub Method extensively as well, refueling from training with a mix of prison chow and "spread" (Top Ramen, Cheez-Its, chips and other ingredients mixed together with hot water in a garbage bag, which then expanded into a large edible mass). For extra protein, I bribed the houseman of the cell block with boxing lessons in return for the extra cartons of skim milk that he held back for himself.

You can find the original Dub Method program in its entirety here:

https://wildhuntconditioning.myshopify.com/products/the-dub-method

53. The History Of The Heelhook

The heel hook, a particularly dangerous lower body submission utilized in grappling and mixed martial arts, has seen a resurgence in recent years thanks to athletes and coaches like Dean Lister, John Danaher and Garry Tonon. It is most often conducted by using the legs to entangle and control the opponent's lower body while their foot is twisted by a leverage point on the heel, using the whole body to generate force. The result is a severe medial torque on the ankle, the force of which translates up into the knee with the potential for inflicting devastating injury. Today the technique is a common sight from ADCC Submission Grappling Championships to UFC fights, however its origins are clouded in half truths and misinformation.

What we can say for certain is that the heel hook was not invented by the Gracie Family as some claim, nor by Vale Tudo fighter Ivan Gomes as others believe. In fact, the heel hook was being used by American catch wrestlers long before the Gracie's even started grappling in the early 20th century. However the story of the heel hook extends back much further than most realize, at least as far back as Ancient Greece, with a man named Halter.

Born in Cilicia, a region on the coast of modern day Turkey known for producing the Mediterranean's most successful and infamous pirates, Halter was a rather small man without any notable physical characteristics. Despite his diminutive build Halter aspired to become a great Pankratist (an Ancient Hellenic Mixed Martial Artist fighter), however in an era without weight classes he frequently found himself being smashed in training by larger opponents. Determined to achieve his dream, he travelled to the Temple of Delphi and asked the Oracle how he could triumph over larger, stronger and more athletic opponents.

The Oracle replied: 'By being trampled upon.'

Halter was confused and discouraged, but he continued to train whilst pondering the Oracle's words. Some time later Halter had a fight, and he found himself underneath his opponent clutching the man's foot by the heel as the larger man 'trampled' on him. In that moment Halter understood the Oracles words, for the one who attacks his opponents legs must place himself underneath them where they risk being 'trampled'. Halter secured the submission, finishing the heel hook and getting his opponent to concede. From there he would go on to become a leg lock specialist with many heel hook finishes, completing his career years later with an undefeated record.

54. The History Of The Deadlift

Known by many to be the truest indicator of overall strength, the history of the deadlift is commonly said to date back to around 1910. However this is not true. While Hermann Görner, a German strongman, brought the 'barbell deadlift' into the public spotlight in 1910's, the lift itself dates back much further. French strongman and wrestler Apollon the Mighty performed a variety of strength feats including deadlifts using a giant barbell he had made out of a train axle, using giant railcar wheels for plates in the 19th century, while Scottish Highlanders frequently deadlifted stones by attached iron rings. Going back even earlier, medics in the Ancient Roman army trained the deadlift to prevent back injuries that accompanied the loading and carrying of fallen soldiers, while in Ancient Greece athletes trained their hamstrings by performing straight leg deadlifts with stone weights called 'halteres', and soldiers in the Ancient Egyptian army performed deadlifts with large bags of sand.

However the history of the deadlift goes back even earlier than that, all the way back to the beginning: the earliest stone lifting contests. It doesn't matter whether you're lifting a barbell or a stone from the ground: a deadlift is a deadlift. As such it's not possible to provide a date of origin but stone lifting, and therefore deadlifting, has been present in the tribal roots of virtually every culture and likely was even practiced by Neanderthals. Such feats of strength were not only used to garner prestige but also to measure and quantify a man's ability to work and contribute to his society. In Viking Age Iceland, a society built around warriors and fisherman, lifting stones were used to determine a man's strength level (and therefore his might as a warrior and use in loading large catches of fish):

-amlóði ("useless") at 23 kg (50.7 pounds)
-hálfdrættingur ("weakling") at 54 kg (119 pounds)
-hálfsterkur ("half strength") at 100 kg (220.5 pounds)
-fullsterkur ("full strength") weighing 154 kg (339.5 pounds)

The heaviest deadlift currently on record is 501 kg (1,104.5 lb), achieved by Hafþór Júlíus Björnsson.

55. Rough And Tumble

In rural areas of America during the 18th and 19th centuries, there existed a form of fighting known as 'Rough and Tumble'. Common among the poor, there were virtually no rules: wrestling, striking (both standing and on the ground) and all types of submission holds were permitted, as was biting, strikes to the groin and eye-gouging. When used to settle a dispute in the manner of a duel, combatants could agree to fight by prizefighting rules or opt to go "rough and tumble", with victors often becoming local heroes. The barbaric fighting style was most common throughout the South and in the working class communities throughout Kentucky, Virginia and Pennsylvania.

The savagery exhibited by Rough and Tumble fighters was shocking to European observers, and an act passed by the Virginia Assembly in 1752 refers to these men by stating "many mischievous and ill disposed persons have of late, in a malicious and barbarous manner, maimed, wounded, and defaced, many of his majesty's subjects".

Philip Vickers Fithian would describe Rough and Tumble in 1774 as follows:

"...like prize-fighting, two men would meet at a space, surrounded by a cheering and typically inebriated crowd, and start off by boxing. However, the fights would quickly deviate from standard pugilistic decorum, for the rules that kept boxing confined to rules of engagement, Rough and Tumble fights were truly anything goes. When one man would go to the ground, the other man could kick, stomp, strike, or gouge. In Rough and Tumble fights, there were no-holds barred as part of the 'gentlemanly' agreement. The only thing that was not permitted was the use of weapons, although that did not deter many fighters from turning their own bodies into weapons".

56. Brazilian Jiujitsu

Mitsuyo Maeda was one of Kodokan Judo's top groundwork experts. Trained by Judo's founder Kano Jigoro, he left Japan in his mid-twenties to tour the world giving demonstrations and accepting challenge fights with boxers, wrestlers and strongmen (despite being under 5'5" and weighing only 140 lbs.). In 1917, a 14-year old named Carlos Gracie would watch one of these demonstrations at the Da Paz Theatre in Belem, Brazil, and decided to learn Judo. He and his family would go on to develop ne-waza, the ground fighting aspect of Judo, into a more comprehensive system known today known as Brazilian Jiujitsu

(BJJ).

At the practical level, BJJ demonstrates that a smaller, weaker person can successfully defend themselves against a bigger and stronger opponent by using leverage, technique and movement to put their opponent on the ground before applying any number of pins, chokeholds or joint locks. Unusually among martial arts, there is also a gradient in the application of force, allowing the infliction of everything from gentle restraint to devastating injury.

Born in a world of challenge fights between martial artists of different disciplines that would eventually evolve into the mixed martial arts of today, few understood the power of Brazilian Jiu Jitsu. This all changed on November 12, 1993 when the Ultimate Fighting Championship held their first event. The martial arts world had long debated which styles were most effective in real world application and many watched curiously as martial artists of all styles gathered to battle each other in a cage without weight classes, drug testing or time limits. At the end of this clash of imposing styles and martial artists, the last man standing was a 175 lbs Brazilian man in white gi named Royce Gracie.

“The deepest benefits of Jiu Jitsu come off the mat. It encourages a world-view based upon the idea of rational problem solving. Jiu Jitsu is all about solving problems that are rapidly changing under stress”. - John Danaher

57. The Huśafell Stone

The Húsafell Stone is a lifting stone located in Huśafell, Iceland weighing 409 lbs. (186 kg) kept near a sheep pen built by a man named Snorri Björnsson over two hundred years ago. The stone has long been used as a test of strength by the locals. Those who could lift the stone up to knee level were labeled amlóði ("useless" or “lazybones”) while those who could lift it up to the waist were labeled hálfsterkur ("half strength"). To be labeled fullsterkur ("full strength"), one had to lift the stone to chest level and then carry it around the perimeter of the sheep pen.

The Húsafell Stone has become an iconic object in the world of strength sports, with the actual stone being used in competition in the 1992 World's Strongest Man competition. Replicas of the same size and weight are still used in competitions around the world and in the 2017 Iceland's Strongest Man competition, Hafþór Júlíus Björnsson (the elite strongman and actor who portrayed The Mountain in the 'Game of Thrones' series, mentioned above as the deadlift world record holder) carried the stone for 90 meters, shattering the previous record of 70 meters.

58. Persistence Hunting

Persistence hunting is a hunting technique in which hunters who are slower than their prey over short distances use a combination of endurance running and tracking to run down their quarry. The strategy has been used by hunter gatherers since mankind's earliest days as well as canids such as wolves and African wild dogs. Even into modern times this practice was associated with hunter gatherer culture such as the San Bushmen of the Kalahari or the Tarahumara of northern Mexico. There was even a family who fled into the frozen Siberian wilderness to escape religious persecution in 1936, who survived for 40 years by clothing themselves in bark, using stone tools and persistence hunting to feed themselves.

As the best endurance runners on the planet, human beings are uniquely suited to persistence hunting, which allows us to overcome larger, faster and more dangerous animals. This ability originates in a unique combination of anatomical and physiological features including but not limited to our bipedalism, sweat glands, hairlessness and our ability to track prey effectively with our eyes. At some point early in our history humans figured out that while it was a bad idea to try to fight a large animal head on, chasing it over several miles of broken ground while guiding it away from shelter, shade and water until it collapsed from exhaustion was a more prudent route to success. At that point, it was a simple matter to dispatch the animal with an arrow at close range, the thrust of a spear or even simply a knife.

In his book 'Why We Run: A Natural History', Bernd Heinrich writes:

"We are a different sort of predator. We can't outsprint most prey. We are psychologically evolved to pursue long-range goals, because through millions of years that is what we on average had to do in order to eat. To us, even an old deer that had not yet been caught would have required a very long chase. It would have required strategy, knowledge, and persistence. Those hominids who didn't have the taste for the long hunt, as such, perhaps for its own sake, would very seldom have been successful. They left fewer descendants.

59. Why Are Belt Buckles Awarded For Completing Ultramarathons?

Though occasionally debated, it can be reasonably assumed that the practice of awarding a belt buckle upon completion of an ultramarathon started with the Western States Endurance Run. The history of the race begins in 1955 with the first Western States Trail Ride: Wendell Robie, an outdoorsman from Auburn, CA got into an argument with another man about whether or not a horseback rider could cover 100 miles in a day. Told it was impossible, he set out to prove it could be done on a historic trail from the 1800's that ran through the little old gold towns between Lake Tahoe and Auburn, California and crossed over the crest of the Sierra Nevada Mountains. Robie then organized, and tied for first place in, the first ever Western States Trail Ride, finishing in 23 hours and 45 minutes. As with many traditional horse races, the prize for completion was a belt buckle, and the horse race went on to become extremely popular, with actor Clark Gable serving as a judge one year.

During the race of 1973 a man named Gordy Ainsleigh attempted the ride only for his horse to fall lame 30 miles in, forcing him to walk the rest of the distance. This inspired Gordy and the next year, he decided to RUN the horse race on foot. It was said that no one could run the trail in under 24 hours but Gordy believed otherwise. Gordy trained hard and a few days before his attempt, he rode his dirt bike to different parts of the course to plant caches of Gatorade. On the morning of the race Gordy took off and the horses soon passed him, but he before long began passing THEM as they grew tired. By the time Gordy reached Last Chance at Devil's Thumb, the heat had climbed to 107 degrees, but he ate a can of peaches and continued on.

In the end Gordy finished the race in 23 hours and 42 minutes, somersaulting across the finish line, and was awarded a custom silver belt buckle made by Comstock Heritage in Reno. Today the Western States Endurance Run uses the same route and aid stations and awards belt buckles to those who finish, with the coveted silver belt buckle for those who do so in under 24 hours.

60. Where Does The Marathon Come From?

In 490 BC the massive army of the Persian Emperor Darius invaded the Greek mainland, aiming to conquer Athens in the knowledge that the rest of Greece would fall. Faced with conquest and destruction at the hands of an unstoppable foe, Athens sent their greatest runner Pheidippides to Sparta to request the aid of the legendary Spartan army. However Pheidippides arrived during the festival of Carneia, a 'sacrosanct period of peace', and was informed that the Spartan army could not march to war until the full moon rose in ten days: the Athenians would have to hold out at Marathon for the time being, reinforced by only 1,000 hoplites from the small city of Plataea.

The Persian ships landed at the Bay of Marathon, and it was there the Athenians chose to make their stand. After a five day showdown across the plains of Marathon, the Athenian general ordered a full charge against the Persian line with two simple words: "at them". His armored men charged across the plains of Marathon through a hail of arrows and smashed into the Persians. Having reinforced his flanks at the expense of leaving the center weaker, the enemy pushed the weaker center inward only for the stronger flanks to collapse inwards, enveloping them. The Persian army broke and fled towards their ships and thousands were slaughtered.

Knowing the whole of Greece was on the brink of panic and chaos in the face of the Persian invasion, the runner Pheidippides ran the entire 25 miles from Marathon back to Athens without stopping, dropping his weapons and clothing to discard as much weight as possible. Upon arrival he exclaimed "we have won!", before collapsing and dying.

While many people know that the marathon originated with this battle, few people know of Pheidippides and even fewer know that in reality his accomplishment is far greater than running a marathon: he ran about 150 miles in two days in order to solicit the help of the Spartans before the battle, and then ran back. He then ran the 25 miles to Marathon for the battle and then back again to Athens to announce the Greek victory, before dying. All in all, he ran over 350 miles in the midst of the largest war the world had ever seen.

Over the years, the distance of the Olympic marathon event has subtly changed, growing over time:

•1896: 24.85 miles
•1900: 25.02 miles
•1904: 24.85 miles
•1906: 26.01 miles
•1908: 26.22 miles
•1912: 24.98 miles
•1920: 26.56 miles
•1924-Present: 26.22 miles

61. The Arm Strength Of English Longbowmen

The arms of Medieval English archers were so strong that their bones actually changed shape. Archeologists have found that the bones in the left arms, left shoulders and right fingers of the skeletons of English longbowmen had actually remodeled to become larger and denser after years of shooting giant longbows, as well as evidence that the muscles they anchored were equally overdeveloped. These archers began using the longbow in childhood, and by the time they were adults they could expertly draw and shoot these bows, something that even top modern weightlifters struggle to do. The English longbow itself was over 6 feet long, made from solid yew wood and required up to 150 pounds of force just to draw. Known as the 'medieval machine gun', it had an effective range of up to 350 yards and the ability to penetrate all but the very best steel armor of the day.

62. Neanderthals Ate Ketogenic And Carnivorous Diet?

A recent study from the Max Planck Institute for Evolutionary Anthropology suggests some Neanderthals survived almost entirely on meat. Analysis of a 50,000 year old Neanderthal tooth from Spain found zinc-64 (the form of zinc found in animal muscle) but almost no zinc-66 (the form found in plants), results which were echoed at eight other sites. Shockingly, the levels of animal sourced zinc-64 were even higher in these samples than those found in obligate carnivores like big cats.

Additional skeletal evidence suggests that the more robust livers and urinary systems of Neanderthals may have allowed them to process protein more efficiently, allowing them to avoid the symptoms of protein overconsumption seen in modern humans, and if they weren't consuming plants (the source of nearly all carbohydrates) then they must have been utilizing fat as their primary fuel source, meaning these Neanderthals were on a ketogenic diet. This information was surprising as Neanderthals were not very different from us, yet the evidence indicates that they possessed physiological adaptations which allowed them to survive on a carnivorous diet with greater efficiency than modern human populations.

63. The Farmer Who Won A 544 Mile Race In Work Boots And Overalls

Sixty-one year old Australian farmer Cliff Young won a 544 mile ultramarathon wearing work boots and overalls, having left his dentures behind because he said they rattled when he ran. Young, a sheep farmer, began the 1983 Westfield Sydney to Melbourne Ultramarathon at a slow, steady pace that initially saw him fall behind the other competitors. However at night, when the other runners stopped to sleep, Cliff kept going. Prior to the race, he had commented that he could go a long time without rest because he was accustomed to chasing sheep for two to three days nonstop. In the end he would run continuously for five straight days, later claiming he simply pretended he was chasing sheep, winning the race by more than 10 hours and breaking the all-time record for a run between Sydney and Melbourne.

Upon being awarded the $10,000 prize, Young said he hadn't even known there was prize money. He then divided the money evenly between the other competitors, taking none for himself.

64. The Maasai

The Maasai are a tribe of lion hunters from Africa who have mastered plyometrics training in a way that modern fitness coaches have not. Most of the fitness community is doing it incorrectly. Plyometric training does NOT consist of deep box jumps and weighted jump training.

The goal of plyometrics exercises is to generate maximum power in a short amount of time, and this is achieved by minimizing the amount of time that the feet are in contact with the ground during each jump or explosive movement, with a recommended maximum ground contact time of 0.2 seconds per jump. The jumping style of the Maasai involves a series of quick, explosive jumps in which the heels never touch the ground. Maasai jumping contests, known as "adumu" or
"Aigus". Were traditionally performed by young Maasai warriors as a display of strength, agility and endurance, this jumping technique is thought to have developed a way for the Maasai to train for hunting and warfare, as it improves leg strength, power, and endurance.

Studies have shown that Maasai warriors who regularly participate in jumping contests have higher bone density, muscle mass and lower body fat than other individuals. This is due to the repeated impact of forces and eccentric contractions involved in jumping. Additionally, the Maasai jumping technique has been found to improve balance, proprioception and coordination

65. The Barkley Marathons

The Barkley Marathons were started by a man named Gary "Lazarus Lake" Cantrell. Their origins date back to 1977 when Martin Luther King's assassin James Earl Ray, escaped from a Tennessee prison. Ray was recaptured after a couple days, having only made it 8 miles through the Tennessee backwoods. Upon hearing this, Lazarus responded simply, "Hell, I coulda done at least a hundred"

And with that, the seed of one of the most brutal races in human history was planted. Only 40 runners are invited to participate each year, mailing in an application and paying a non-refundable registration fee of $1.60. When and how to apply is secret. Participants are also expected to pay another fee, usually in the form of an article of clothing such as a white shirt or socks. Those participating for the first time, or "Barkley virgins" as Cantrell called them, are also asked to bring a license plate from their state or country. The race itself consists of multiple loops on a route running twenty plus miles through the Cumberland Mountains in Frozen Head State Park. The unmarked route has a total elevation gain of 60,000 ft. Equivalent to climbing Mt. Everest twice. The start of the race has been described as such:

"Between Midnight and Noon, usually on a Saturday. However racers are never told when the race will officially start. The only indication they receive for the start time is by Cantrell blowing a conch shell to signify that the race will start exactly one hour from that time. The start of the race is then signaled by Cantrell lighting a cigarette. Participants then have 60 hours to complete the race."

In addition, between nine and eleven of Lazarus' favorite books are hidden along the route (one year they were porno magazines) and the participants must find each book and remove the page corresponding to the number on their race bib in order to finish. There are no aid stations and only two locations to get water on the route, with only twelve hours to complete each loop.

In the entire history of the race only 18 people have ever finished, including Lazarus himself.

66. Six Facts About Runners In The Aztec Empire

At the peak of their power the Aztecs controlled a vast empire in Central Mexico. From the great temples and floating gardens of their highland capital, east to the Gulf of Mexico and west to the Pacific Ocean, their subjects offered tribute. And it was their runners that held it all together. Here are six facts you probably didn't know:

1. Aztec Emperors maintained an elite corps of runners to carry messages throughout the empire in relays of approx. 3.6 miles. This network of messengers could carry a message 300 miles in a single day, and was a key factor behind their military power.

2. These elite runners were selected at a young age and trained under supervision of the priests in the sacred precinct. In order to strengthen their legs and lungs, the boys were trained meticulously, including runs up and down the steps of the Great Temple.

3. Aztec runners supplemented with spirulina, formed into little cakes that were said to smell like cheese, and fueled for their runs with superfoods like amaranth, quinoa and chia seeds.

4. These runners carried government messages, military intelligence and acted as spies. They even transported goods like ice, snow and ocean fish great distances so their rulers could enjoy fresh luxuries from faraway lands.

5. During the New Fire ceremony, a high ranking victim was sacrificed and a fire was lit inside their chest. This fire was then used to light torches that were carried by the runners to the many

temples throughout the empire.

6. Running was considered a military activity and skilled messengers were often promoted to leadership roles. Running was so revered that it even had its own god, Painal.

67. Māori Strength Training

The Māori people of New Zealand are known as some of the strongest people in history. They engaged in a variety of activities that prioritized strength, such as fishing, hunting and warfare. Traditional Māori training methods focused on building functional strength to support these activities, much like an early form of tactical conditioning.

1. The Māori practiced strongman training with large logs and stones to build functional strength.

2. Another training method involves training using the taiaha, a traditional Māori staff weapon made from whalebone or hardwood that was used to build upper body strength in addition to martial strength.

3. Their favorite form of cardio was rowing. As skilled seafarers, the Māori rowed canoes called waka over the open ocean for weeks, developing a high degree of endurance despite their inclination towards large, muscular builds.

Finally, the Māori practiced mamau, a form of wrestling that was often used to settle disputes and was an important part of Māori culture.

68. Three Training Methods Of Inca Runners

The chasqui runners of the Inca Empire lived and trained in the

Andes mountains, where extremely high elevation (over 20,000 feet) and rugged terrain present a unique challenge to physical performance. To cope, Inca runners developed unique training methods and nutrition that allowed them to excel in this harsh environment. With these training and nutrition techniques, elite messenger runners carried messages and goods throughout the empire, over footpaths and rope bridges high in the Andes mountains, often covering over 100 miles of steep terrain in a day.

Training methods:

1. Altitude training: many of the Inca cities and settlements were located above 10,000 feet. As a result, their bodies were already adapted to the thin air and reduced oxygen levels that come with high altitude. However runners would also train at even HIGHER elevations to further improve their endurance in this low-oxygen environment.
2. Weighted Carries: Inca runners would often carry heavy loads of food, water and goods over long distances. They also carried stones up inclines to build their strength, endurance and mental toughness.
3. Interval training: this involved alternating between running at a fast pace for a short period and a slower pace for a longer period. By rotating between high intensity and low intensity running, Inca runners were able to improve their overall cardiovascular fitness, speed and endurance.

Diet:

Primary energy sources were potatoes, quinoa, purple corn, lupin bean, maca root, lucuma fruit and sacha inchi (known as 'Inca peanuts'). Primary protein sources were meat of llama, alpaca, deer and Guinea pig. Blue algae and seaweed were consumed as health supplements, while coca leaf was chewed to relieve symptoms of altitude sickness, suppress appetite and maintain alertness on long runs.

69. The Arctic Training And Diet Of The Inuit

The Inuit people are known for surviving the harsh arctic environment and hunting polar bears with wooden bows. What many don't know is that they also have a rich tradition of strength training going back thousands of years. These are 5 training methods they used to survive in the most hostile environment on earth:

1. One-foot high kick: This movement requires the player to use a running start to jump and kick a hanging ball on foot.
2. Head Pull: two people lie belly-down on the ground, pull each other's heads, connected by a leather strap, and try to move the opponent across a line
3. One Arm Reach: requires you to post your whole weight on one hand long enough to reach up to touch a hanging ball.
4. Leg Wrestling: lying on their backs side by side, heads in opposite directions, competitors link their inside legs and attempt to flip each other.
5. Finger pull: two players sit facing each other with their feet touching. Each player grips a pair of small wood handles and tries to out-pull and outlast the other.
6. Bonus: Alaskan High Kick: similar to the one-foot high kick, but the Alaskan high kick requires the player to jump and kick from a starting position on the ground.

Additionally, the Inuit have traditionally survived off an almost entirely animal based diet revolving around seal, whale, caribou, birds and fish. Living in an area devoid of edible plants, the primary source of both carbohydrates and vitamin C, the Inuit have adapted to relying on fat as a primary fuel source (making them a common focus for ketogenic dietary studies) and obtaining vitamin C from the skin and organs of marine mammals like narwhal and whale.

70. The Ultramarathon Monks Of Japan

In the mountains of Japan there is an ancient sect of Buddhist monks who believe running a 7 year ultramarathon is the path to enlightenment. The longest and most dangerous endurance trial in the world, it is a pilgrimage known as the 'Kaihōgyō', and the monks believe that those who compete this challenge are born anew, ascending to a state of living sainthood. The practice has been around for over a thousand years however since 1885 only 46 monks have managed to complete the Kaihōgyō, and only two since WW2.

To complete the 7 year challenge one must complete the following every year (while meditating and offering prayers):

•Years 1-3: cover twenty five miles per day for 100 days.

•Years 4-5: cover twenty five miles per day for 200 days.

•Year 6: cover thirty seven miles per day for 100 days.

•Year 7: cover fifty two miles per day for 100 days, followed by twenty five miles per day for another 100 days.

Many who attempt the challenge die, as seen in the many graves and skeletons dotting the route. Participants wear white robes (the color of death) and carry a ritual coin to pay the mythological ferryman to bring them across the River of the Dead in case their attempt ends in death. Their only footwear is sandals made from woven rope and their only protection from the elements is a hat made from woven wood (they can only wear it when it rains). Throughout the challenge, the monks eat a vegetarian diet that consists of fried tofu, rice, vegetables, seaweed and milk. During the 5th year, participants must sit for nine days with zero food and zero sleep, with water brought to them only once a day, while they meditate and pray to their principal deity, the Immovable Wisdom King, a wrathful guardian spirit covered flames, dressed in rags and holding a sword and rope.

By the time one has completed the Kaihogyo, they have covered a distance greater than the circumference of the earth.

CREDITS

Author: James Pieratt

For more, you can find us at:
Website: https://wildhuntconditioning.myshopify.com/pages/links

Instagram: https://www.instagram.com/wildhuntconditioning/?igshid=YmMyMTA2M2Y=

YouTube:
https://youtube.com/channel/UCTgBjdLR9VFgNsidVdBVdng